Is it wrong to dedicate a book to a place? Well, I'm dedicating this book to Anna Maria Island and the Southern gulf coast of Florida. Walking along those shores brings me so much happiness and restores my soul.

KAY'S BOOKS

Find more information on all my books at
kaycorrell.com

COMFORT CROSSING ~ THE SERIES
The Shop on Main - Book One
The Memory Box - Book Two
The Christmas Cottage - A Holiday Novella
(Book 2.5)
The Letter - Book Three
The Christmas Scarf - A Holiday Novella (Book 3.5)
The Magnolia Cafe - Book Four
The Unexpected Wedding - Book Five

The Wedding in the Grove - (a crossover short story
between series - with Josephine and Paul from The
Letter.)

LIGHTHOUSE POINT ~ THE SERIES
Wish Upon a Shell - Book One
Wedding on the Beach - Book Two
Love at the Lighthouse - Book Three
Cottage near the Point - Book Four
Return to the Island - Book Five

INDIGO BAY ~ A multi-author sweet romance series
Sweet Sunrise - Book Three
Sweet Holiday Memories - A short holiday story
Sweet Starlight - Book Nine

Sign up for my newsletter at my website *kaycorrell.com* to make sure you don't miss any new releases or sales.

CHAPTER 1

Tally had a love-hate relationship with the sea. Today it bordered more on the liked-quite-a-bit side of the scale. She stood on the beach at Lighthouse Point on Belle Island. The waves raced up the gentle slope of sand and lapped at her bare feet. This had to be her favorite spot, especially in the early morning hours when all she would pass was an occasional jogger or shell collector. The lighthouse was no longer a functioning lighthouse, but it continued to stand regally over the Florida beach, protecting the inhabitants of the island.

The sky slowly splashed into a wash of muted colors, as if someone had tossed watercolors across the horizon. She reached down and scooped up a handful of dry sand, letting the grains sift slowly through her fingers and into the waves. A lone shell tumbled around her feet, taunting her, but she refused to bend over and pick it up. Town legend held that by throwing a shell into the ocean and making a wish at Lighthouse Point, the wish would come true. Tally knew that whole town lore was a lie, a lie she no longer fell for. Not that she hadn't used that very legend twenty-five years ago when she named her restaurant Magic Cafe. But that had been when she was young and still foolishly believed in all that nonsense.

A lone blue heron flew past her. She watched as it flapped its wings in a rhythmic motion, continuing down the beach until she lost it in the distance. The breeze tossed her gray-sprinkled hair this way and that. The gray she never considered coloring back to its original chestnut brown, there was no time for such frivolities.

She glanced at her watch. It was time to head back to the cafe. It might not open until eleven, but she had a ton of work to do each morning before she unlocked the doors. Plus, this was her monthly get-together with her friends Susan and Julie, a date that was never broken. Her friends would come by for a late lunch and they'd chat and catch up on each other's busy lives. It was a precious few hours each month they would grab out of their single businesswomen lives and just relax.

Tally took one last look out into the ocean and watched the gentle waves roll in, lost in thoughts and memories and her ever-ebbing relationship with the sea. She turned and headed down the beach towards the cafe.

~

Julie Farmington slammed the door to the battered delivery truck. An hour for deliveries, then back to The Sweet Shoppe to open it by seven. She had a girl who helped her in the shop in the mornings, but the girl was kind of hit and miss on showing up. Julie hopped this morning was a hit, not a miss.

A light breeze blew in from the gulf, cooling her flushed face. Owning a bakery wasn't for sissies. She'd already been up for two hours helping her cook, Nancy, with the morning baking and loading up the morning orders. She snatched off the cap she wore for baking, and her long brown hair tumbled down around her shoulders. She reached up and twisted it into a loose knot.

She swung into the van, glancing at the tear in the vinyl seat and wondering if she should duct tape it before it split all the way across. It was just one more thing on her already too long to-do list.

The van ground to life, and she headed towards Belle Island Inn with their daily order. She pulled up to the side door of the quaint inn, and her friend Susan hurried out of the propped-open kitchen door.

"There you are. Let me help you." Susan walked to the back of the van and tugged open the door. "You coming to Tally's later this afternoon?"

"I will. Might be late if Chrissy doesn't show up."

"We've got to find you a more responsible worker." Susan reached for a tray of bread and pastries.

"Once school is out, I'll have more of choice. Always hard to find workers during the school year."

"Tell me about it. I just fired a boy who astounded it wasn't okay for him to miss two days in a row without calling, then showed up to work like nothing happened. Kids these days." Her friend laughed. "I sound like an old lady."

Her friend was anything but an old lady. Susan might be over fifteen years Julie's senior, but she had the energy of ten people and worked tirelessly trying to keep Belle Island Inn afloat. Julie followed Susan into the kitchen and placed her armload of boxes on the counter. Susan's cook bustled in the kitchen getting ready for their breakfast crowd. Julie lifted a hand in greeting, then turned. "I'd better run. I'll see you later at Tally's."

Susan nodded and started unpacking the tray of baked goods. "We'll wait for you if you're late."

Julie headed back to the van, glancing at her watch. She was cutting it close today. She made her regular morning delivery to Magic Cafe, but Tally wasn't there yet. She was probably off on her morning walk. Her friend did love her daily jaunt, only the very worst weather could keep her off the beach.

Julie made a delivery to Good Luck Mart by the bridge. She pulled into the parking lot behind The Sweet Shoppe with five minutes to spare.

"I've got the coffee started, but no helper today. Again. I'll help at the counter as much as I can."

"Thanks, Nancy." Julie headed to the front door, flipped the sign to open, and twisted the lock with a metallic click. She smiled at Dan Smith as he walked into the shop, always her first customer of the day.

"You got those blueberry muffins today?"

"I do. I'll get you one and your coffee."

"Thanks, Julie." Dan slipped into a table in the corner. His table. But then, since he was always the first one here, he'd have his pick of any spot.

Julie squared her shoulders in preparation for another day without enough help, and headed to the display counter to grab Dan's order of his favorite pastry.

Tally filled another shaker with sea salt and set it on the tray. The lunch crowd had died down, and she expected Susan and Julie any minute.

She was glad she'd made the decision, years ago, that the cafe would only serve lunch and dinner. As it was, it was open every day of the week. This at least gave her a brief bit of time to herself in the early mornings, and her monthly get-togethers with her friends were a not-to-be-missed-for-any-reason date on her calendar.

She looked up and saw Julie and Susan crossing the wide deck of the outside seating area of Magic Cafe. They waved to her and sat down at their usual table. Tally finished filling the last shaker and walked over to greet her friends.

"Hope you guys want grouper. I have an extra-large shipment. A group that was scheduled to come tomorrow just canceled. Last minute." Tally slid into a chair across from her friends.

"Grouper sandwich it is, then." Susan set down her menu without even looking at it.

Tally wasn't sure why any of the waitresses gave her friends a menu. It's not like Susan would need it after coming to the cafe for the last seven years, ever since she first moved to the island. And Julie practically grew up here, showing up her first day on the island when she was barely eighteen years old— lost, no job, and not knowing a soul.

"Grouper for me, too. Blackened." Julie handed her menu to the waitress who had brought over sweet tea for the table.

Tally looked over at Julie, marveling at the young woman she'd become. She'd blossomed into a smart, confident business owner and Tally couldn't be prouder of her.

Julie looked up and smiled. "Watcha thinking? I see that look in your eyes."

"Thinking the three of us have come a long way together."

"I don't know what would have happened to me if you hadn't taken me under your wing all those years ago. Given me that room in the storage building. I still kind of miss that place. It was the first time I'd ever had a room of my own in my whole life." Julie leaned back in her chair

"It was pretty sparse." Tally shook her head.

"It was mine. That was all that mattered."

"You had it pretty well all dolled up by the time you moved on." Tally smiled.

"I was so proud of those curtains I made and that old yellow bedspread. I still have it and use it as a beach blanket. Well, I would if, you know, I ever had time to go to the beach."

Tally leaned forward. "That reminds me. My manager has a niece who's moving to the island. Needs a job. Good worker. I said you could use someone, and I told her to drop by to talk to you."

"That would be great, thanks. The shop finally makes enough so I can afford to hire more workers, but I just can't find good help. Except for Nancy. She's great."

"I miss having you as our baker at Magic Cafe,

7

but since I can buy my bread and pastries from you now, it all worked out."

"I've been getting some catering business, too. I'm also hoping to do more wedding cakes."

Susan set her glass on the table. "I've told our wedding planner at the inn to recommend you. We're really working on ramping up the wedding business this summer. We do have a few booked in June. Just need to get our name out there as a wedding destination. Jamie's been working on it."

"That son of yours is a hard worker." Tally had a momentary twinge of longing, a vague yearning of a dream long ago of sharing a business with a family member. That would never happen, of course.

"Jamie *is* a hard worker. I don't know what I'd do without him. We still haven't turned the inn around. It's a daily struggle. It has to work, though. It's Jamie's whole life. Well, mine too, I guess. But I think Jamie wants to make it a success to make a point. Prove he can do it." Susan looked out at the ocean. "He wants his stepfather to see we've been fine without him, even though the man is no longer his stepfather."

"Nor is he your husband any longer," Julie chimed in.

"Thank goodness. Even though the inn is grueling work hours, I love it. I love running it. And you both have been such good sources of help and inspiration. You practically adopted me when I moved here to help Jamie run the inn. I can't believe it's been almost seven years."

"To us." Julie raised her glass.

"To us," Tally and Susan joined in.

Tally looked at her friends, a strange mix, each born in a different decade. But, somehow, they made it work. Friends through it all, ready in an instant if any of the trio needed help, advice, comfort, or the occasional glass of medicinal Chardonnay or two.

Tally was lucky, she was, she knew that. She might not have a family anymore, but she had these two women. They were as close to family as a person could get without being blood-related.

CHAPTER 2

Reed Newman watched out the side window of the town car as the driver headed over the bridge to Belle Island. What was he doing here? What had possessed him to think this was a good idea, to travel completely across the country?

A vacation.

Like he even knew what that was.

But he had a month off, courtesy of his boss. To be honest, his boss had insisted. Reed had briefly toyed with sitting in his Seattle home the entire time, to spite his boss's order or because it just seemed like an enormous effort to plan a vacation, one of the two.

After three days of stewing in his house, he'd switched on the television, a rarity in and of itself. A program of best beaches to visit in the U.S. flashed on the screen. He watched as the show jumped from a honky-tonk boardwalk beach to a peaceful island on the gulf in southern Florida.

He'd flipped open his laptop, searched for the island, and booked a month's stay at Belle Island Inn. It was the most spontaneous decision he'd made in years.

One he was regretting right now.

The driver pulled up in front of a large shingle-sided inn with a wide porch sprawling across the length of the building. Reed climbed out of the car, and the driver handed him his suitcase.

"Thanks." Reed slipped the man a tip on top of the fee he'd paid to be driven from the Sarasota airport. An airport that had taken two plane changes, a book he wasn't really reading, and countless cups of coffee to reach from Seattle.

A young couple came out the door with a small boy skipping by the man's side. The boy looked up, and the man leaned down and swooped the child up into his arms. The boy laughed, and the woman smiled and rested her hand on the man's arm.

Reed paused, debating flagging the driver and heading back home. Was it going to be an inn full of happy families? Romantic couples? He sure hadn't done his research this time. This is why he should never make spontaneous decisions. Ever.

A young man in a yellow shirt came walking up to the car. His shirt was embroidered with *Belle Island Inn*.

Tell me yellow is not going to be the shirt color of all the workers at the inn.

"Can I get your bags for you?" The young man asked.

"No, I'm fine. Thanks anyway."

The late afternoon sun danced among the fronds of the palm trees lining the drive. The town car pulled away and Reed climbed the steps, passing the happy family with a brief nod, and headed in for his month-long sentence.

Susan looked up from the reception desk to see a man stride into the lobby of the inn. He was dressed in business casual, had an air of solitude wrapped firmly around him, and looked distinctly out of place.

"May I help you?"

The man crossed the lobby and came up to the desk, setting his suitcase on the floor beside him. He reached into his pocket and fished out his wallet. "Newman. Reed Newman."

"Mr. Newman. Glad to have you stay with us." Susan coaxed the cranky computer to pull up the reservation. It didn't seem very happy to comply with her command, because it flickered once then slowly— oh, so slowly—surrendered the information. "Ah, you're here for the month. The corner suite, top level. That's a wonderful room. Great view."

The man nodded, pulled out his credit card, and handed it to her. She ran it, thankful the card reader had a better attitude than the computer, at least for today.

"We have a restaurant that has a buffet breakfast. We do box lunches you can order the night before if you want one any day. The dining room is open every night except Monday. There are a lot of other places to eat here during your stay. I can recommend some."

"Are they within walking distance?"

"Some are, but we have a free trolley that travels the length of the island that you can use if you don't have a car here."

"I don't."

Susan handed the man a trolley stop map with a list of places to eat, public beaches, and other sites of interest.

"Your room is up those stairs, to the left, last door." Susan pointed to the main staircase off the side of the lobby. "I'm sorry, we're having a bit of trouble with the elevator. It should be fixed tomorrow. You'll have to use the stairs for now."

"Not a problem."

Mr. Newman reached for the key and headed across the lobby with brisk, determined steps. She couldn't shake the feeling that he reminded her of a little-lost boy, which was ridiculous because he was a grown man. She watched as he climbed the stairs and disappeared. She wondered what brought him to the inn for a month. They didn't often get month-long visitors. Most people who came to the island for a long stay leased a house or condo. Not that she was complaining. A month-long customer in the off-season was nice. *Every* customer in off-season was nice.

CHAPTER 3

The next morning Reed stood at the french doors to the balcony and stared out at the ocean. The windows were covered with a fine layer of salt, slightly softening the view. The sea here on the gulf was so different from the sea near Seattle, not that he made the drive to the ocean from Seattle anymore.

This sea was calm this morning, almost lake-like. The colors were an amazing shade of turquoise blended to a brilliant green. A low dune ran the length of the inn's property and beyond. A young man was starting to put up a few rows of lounge chairs and umbrellas on the gently sloping beach.

He sipped his coffee, which was an unusually good blend. He hadn't expected that from a hotel room coffeemaker. The only downside was the yellow mug emblazoned with *Belle Island Inn*.

He'd been glad to see that the woman checking

him in yesterday had on a light blue Belle Island Inn shirt. So yellow wasn't the color for everything here. Thank goodness.

But the mug still bugged him. Stupid yellow mug.

He watched as a bare chested, barefoot runner jogged past. An older lady with a bright, floral cover-up strolled along with a red bucket. She stopped every so often, plucked a shell, look at it carefully to see if it made the cut, then dropped it into her pail or tossed it back on the beach.

They had a purpose.

Exercise.

Shells.

What was he going to do for a month at the beach with no work to do? What had he been thinking? He'd picked a sleepy little island in southern Florida in the off-season, after the snowbirds had left to go back to their various states, after spring break rush was over, before summer season began.

So, really? What was he going to do with himself, well, besides walk everywhere? He'd been careful to choose a place where he could get around without a car. That was a necessity now.

He opened the door and stepped out on the balcony. There wasn't much privacy, but it did hold a comfortable-looking pair of bar-height chairs and a table. He sat on one of the chairs, pleased how it put him high enough he wasn't just staring into the balcony railing. The outdoor furniture design showed a thoughtfulness he appreciated. The planks of the balcony were a worn gray color, the paint smoothed into almost non-existence by the sand and wind. After sitting outside for a few minutes, his skin felt vaguely sticky. He'd forgotten about that, the syrupy feeling of the sea air and humidity when the breeze wasn't chasing it away.

He sat on the balcony for he didn't know how long. He couldn't remember the last time he'd just… sat. He finished his coffee and headed inside to go downstairs and grab some breakfast.

After that, he didn't know what the heck he was going to do with his day. And the twenty-something days after that…

Julie's on-again-off-again worker had actually shown up today and was handling the morning customers with Nancy. Julie always liked to have at least two morning workers plus Nancy on the weekends and during the summer months, but occasionally she would treat herself to a morning off after her deliveries during the slow season.

She decided to walk from her cottage to the inn and see if she could persuade Susan to play hooky for a bit and take a long beach walk. They hadn't done that in a very long time.

She closed the door to her small cottage. It wasn't

19

on the beach, of course, she'd never be able to afford that. It was a tiny, two bedroom home inland, not that the island was wide. The widest point of the island was only a mile across so you were never very far from the beach or the bayside. She actually had a small view of the bay from the widow's walk the previous owner had built on the corner of the back of the house. She'd placed a reading chair and a small table in that cozy space, and it had quickly become her favorite spot in her house.

And the best thing about the cottage? It was hers. All hers. She'd worked long and hard to buy it and the bakery. Five years ago she'd finally been able to scrape together a down payment and had found her home. It was serendipity as far as she was concerned. She never wanted to leave, it was her dream home. Oh, it had needed a lot of work. *A lot of work*. Which was why she'd even been able to afford it. She'd done most of the renovations herself, refinishing the old wooden plank floors and painting walls. Jamie's friend Harry —who seemed to know everything there was to know about repairs—had helped her with some updated plumbing. She'd cleared the overgrown yard and planted a small flower garden. She'd painted the outside of the house a creamy yellow color with white shutters and doors. She was proud of how all the hard work she'd put into the cottage had turned it into a real home.

She would never have imagined when she stepped

onto Belle Island eighteen years ago that she would come this far. Well, to be honest, the bank owned most of her home and the bakery, but she faithfully paid both loans off each month.

Landing on Belle Island had been such a fortuitous coincidence. She'd landed here because she'd bought a bus ticket the day she turned eighteen and it had taken her this far, to Belle Island, so she'd gotten off the bus with her one small bag and twenty dollars to her name. She'd slept that night against a storage building near the beach. Tally found her the next morning and gave her a job at Magic Cafe and a room in that very storage building.

Julie had been so sure her life would fall apart like it always had, bursting into flames and taking her with it down some dark pathway. But day by day, Tally's kindness and her own hard work had taken her out of her nightmare life and into the peaceful existence she craved now, one that allowed for beach walks with her friend.

Julie climbed the stairs from the beach to the large deck that spread across the back of the inn. She headed inside to find Susan.

"Hi, Jules." Jamie stood behind the reception desk.

"Hey, Jamie. I'm looking for your mom. Trying to steal her away for a walk."

"Good idea. She's in the kitchen, I think."

"How have you been?" Julie stopped at the desk. "I haven't seen you in a while."

"I've been busy. Trying to spruce up the inn before the busy season. Did Mom tell you that we've booked a couple of weddings? Hoping that works out. Coming up soon we even have a full inn for a weekend due to a party. Busy time for off-season."

"Does sound busy." Julie knew Susan and Jamie worked long hours keeping the inn running. A few times in the past it had looked like they would lose it, but somehow they always managed to squeak by. Julie didn't know what Susan would do without the inn. It almost seemed like the inn was part of Susan, like the bakery was part of her, and Magic Cafe was part of Tally.

Julie headed to the kitchen and found Susan standing at a counter with a stack of vendor orders and a calculator in front of her. "How about you take a break from that and come walk with me on the beach?"

"I really should figure this out. I think we got shorted on our order." Susan pushed back a lock of curly red hair, the same shade of golden red that her son sported, only Susan's had a strand or two of gray threaded through it.

"Just a little break? It will do you good. You'll come back all refreshed. Probably find the error right away," Julie wheedled.

Dorothy, a woman who had worked at the inn

since before Julie arrived on the island, came into the kitchen. She usually worked the reception desk and probably knew more about the inn than any other person. She'd worked for Jamie's uncle, who had owned the inn before Susan. Dorothy had been employed here since she'd been a young girl, and she was probably in her fifties now. "Jamie said you're taking Susan on a walk. Great idea. She could use the break."

Susan grinned. "Okay, okay. You all win. A short one. It will do me good to get out of here."

They strolled through the lobby and out onto the deck. "Oh, wait. Let me go back and get my sunglasses. Meet you on the beach."

"Okay, but don't get sucked back into work." Julie grinned.

"I won't. Probably."

Julie stood at the bottom of the deck stairs and kicked off her sandals. A lone man approached with what Julie could only call *dress* shorts and a collared knit shirt that looked like it had been ironed, for pete's sake. She looked down at her worn shorts and her t-shirt that proclaimed Belle Island the friendliest town on the gulf, complete with a strawberry stain on the front from the scones she'd made this morning. She scooted to one side of the stairs for him to pass. As she did, she looked up into the most startling blue eyes she'd ever seen. Eyes filled to their depths with... what? Sadness? Loneliness? Her breath caught for a moment before she told herself to quit being a ninny bug, as Tally would say when she thought someone was being silly.

"Excuse me." He nodded at her and climbed the stairs.

She turned to glance over her shoulder. Goosebumps ran up her arms and she rubbed them quickly. Susan hurried down the stairs and looked at her closely. "You okay?"

"Yes. I…" Julie shook her head.

"Did you meet Mr. Newman?"

"Who?"

"The man who just passed you."

"Yes. No. I mean… who is he?"

"Reed Newman. Our month-long visitor."

"He's—well, he needs to find some beach clothes for one thing." *That was what she chose to say to her friend about this man? His clothes?*

"He's from Seattle. Not sure if he's here on business or pleasure. Pleasure, I'd guess. He mentioned he didn't have a car, so it's not like he can travel into Sarasota for work or anything."

"His eyes…" Julie stared up the empty stairway.

"They are sad, aren't they? He looks a little lost."

"I don't know. There was just something about him." Julie turned to her friend. "I'm being foolish. Let's go on our walk."

The two friends linked arms and headed down the beach.

Reed walked into the lobby, then couldn't help himself. He turned around and walked back onto the deck. The woman in the stained t-shirt and the inn owner were walking down the beach, arm-in-arm in that comfortable way women who had been friends for a long time had with each other.

The stained-shirt woman had the most remarkable green eyes, emerald almost. Her skin had been tanned and her face flushed from the heat or a light sunburn, he didn't know. She'd had bare feet with pink toenails, and her fingernails matched. Her long chestnut hair was pulled back into some kind of messy knot.

She looked charming.

Where had the word *charming* come from, and why the heck did he remember every darn detail about her?

Tally looked up towards the end of the lunch shift and saw her friend Paul and his new wife Josephine coming into the cafe. She waved them over to a beachside table. Paul walked up and wrapped his strong arms around her. "Missed you, Tally."

"Did you have a good time in Comfort Crossing?" Tally hugged him back and smiled at Josephine.

"We did. We got more of Josephine's things. We're

25

going to get her all moved in here sooner or later." Paul laughed.

"Of course, Paul would have to clear out another closet and more space for me if I brought even one more item." Josephine's words sounded like she was chiding, but her tone was full of love.

"Jo, I'd buy a whole new house if that's what it takes."

"I love your house. It's quaint and right on the beach by the lighthouse. Who could want more?"

"I'll never want more. I have you." Paul leaned over and kissed his bride.

"Okay, okay, you two. This whole perfect couple thing." Tally grinned. Paul had come to town about twenty-five years ago. He'd opened a gallery in town, the man was a genius with his paints. They'd become friends while they both struggled to keep their businesses going in hard times. Now, thank goodness, times were easier. Barring a disaster like a hurricane coming through, they'd hopefully have some smooth sailing. She winced at the metaphor.

Paul travelled often for gallery shows around the states. Then after one trip, he'd come back and said he was marrying the love of his life, the woman he'd wanted to marry over fifty years ago. They'd found their way back to each other and gotten married. Tally had traveled to Comfort Crossing to go to their wedding, and she couldn't be happier for her friend. Now Josephine had moved to Belle Island. She was a lovely woman and perfect for Paul as far as Tally could tell. At least she'd never seen Paul this happy and content.

Paul held out a chair for Josephine then took the chair beside her. "Can you join us?"

Tally looked around to see how many customers were still left. "I can. For a bit." She sank into a chair across from the couple. They placed their orders and sat quietly chatting.

"Josephine got to see her grandniece and nephew, Bella and Gil. You remember them? You met them at the wedding. We invited them to come down and visit soon. Bella is married now. Gil may come visit with his girlfriend, Madeline."

"I keep expecting to hear about wedding bells for Gil and Madeline, but so far no news. They do make the perfect couple, though." Josephine rested her hand on Paul's arm.

"What's new here on Belle Island?" Paul leaned back in his chair.

"Same old, same old. Not that I'm complaining. It's been nice to have this brief lull between the busy tourist seasons. Traffic has died down since the snowbirds all headed back north. Love the business they bring, just not the traffic."

"Always did like this time of year on the island. And October. The weather is warm, not hot. The island isn't crowded. Slow time of the year for the gallery, but that's okay."

"I saw on the town website you have some new photographer you're showing at the gallery this summer."

"I do. His name is Hunt. He did a series of photos of the destruction along the gulf coast from the last few hurricanes. It's just fascinating. His girlfriend, Keely—she owns Magnolia Cafe up in Comfort Crossing, you'd like her—she wrote up descriptions for each photo he's showing. It's all very moving. I think you'll enjoy it."

"Sounds wonderful. I'll be sure to come by and see it."

Later, Tally watched her friend lead his new wife out of the cafe. He was holding Josephine's hand as if he'd never let go, not that she blamed him. Family. You should always appreciate your time with them. Every single moment.

CHAPTER 4

Reed sat on the comfortable chair on the suite's balcony. The breeze teased his hair, reminding him he need a haircut. He'd have to find a barber on this tiny island who could give him the short, businessman cut he preferred. Of course, that was going to involve finding a barber he could walk to or he'd have to figure out the trolley system... or maybe he should rent a bike for the month. He'd check into that. Something to finally put on his to-do list. He was pretty sure people left their to-do lists at home when they went on vacation, but he felt slightly naked without his list on his phone. He pulled out his cell and started typing. Get haircut. Rent bike. There, that felt better.

He set down his phone and paged through some brochures the young man at the desk had given him about things to do on the island. He didn't know why he called the man young, he was probably close to his own age, but somehow Reed always felt years older than his actual age. Years older.

He opened another brochure and it flipped open to a photo of a lighthouse. He read the blurb about the legend of Lighthouse Point.

Years ago, when the island had first been settled, Margaret Belle's husband, a local fisherman, had been lost as sea. Margaret went to Lighthouse Point on Belle Island and threw a shell into the ocean as she made a wish for her husband to come home safely. Six months to the day he showed up, rescued by another fishing boat. From then on, many residents and visitors to the island have gone to Lighthouse Point, thrown their shells into the sea while making their wishes, and their wishes—big and small—have come true.

Visit Lighthouse Point on Belle Island and make your own wish come true!

He didn't believe in that kind of folklore, but he thought it might be interesting to walk the beach to the lighthouse. It looked like it was only a couple of miles or so down the beach from here. He stood up, went into his room and tossed the brochures on the bed.

He had a mission. A purpose. At least for today.

He'd go see the lighthouse.

Julie walked down the beach toward the lighthouse. This time of year there weren't many people out on Lighthouse Point, but in the summer the island historical society opened up the lighthouse to tours. The parking lot on the nearby public beach would be filled with cars, the beach filled with tourists. For now, she could enjoy the peace and quiet.

Julie didn't believe in the town legend about wishes and Lighthouse Point, but she did dearly love the beach near it. It had been the first beach she'd ever set foot on in her life, all those years ago when she first came to the island.

She walked along the water's edge, letting the gentle waves caress her feet as they rolled onto shore, one after the other. The mid-afternoon sun glinted off the waves and broke into sparkling diamonds across the sea. A light breeze blew her hair away from her shoulders, and she wished she'd thought to tie it back before her walk.

It had been a busy day at The Sweet Shoppe, and she'd met with Heidi, the girl Tally had sent her way. Heidi was eager to start working and was coming early tomorrow morning. It would be nice to have more help. She couldn't continuing doing everything —baking, deliveries, waiting tables, cleaning, marketing, ordering supplies, and every other little job that came up.

Julie wondered if she should try extending store hours in the summer. Right now the bakery closed at two in the afternoon. She wasn't sure they'd get enough customers to justify the cost of staying open later in the day, but she was often tempted to try. Maybe if this new girl worked out she could give it a trial run, but for now she'd stick with the two o'clock closing. There, a decision was made, at least for now.

She stood on the shore and stared out into the ocean. Random thoughts flicked through her mind. Orders that needed to be placed. Tally's birthday coming up—she should talk to Susan about doing something for Tally. The curtains she was sewing for her cottage. All these thoughts surged through her mind. She took a deep breath, quieting her mind, lulling her breathing into matching the pace of the slowly rolling waves. The spring heat washed through her. Yes, this beach, this was her happy place.

She closed her eyes and simply enjoyed the moment.

She opened her eyes and took a few steps back to sit on the dry sand. A lone woman in the distance stood staring at the sea, and then her arm came up and Julie saw her toss a shell into the ocean. Ah, another person sucked into the legend.

A man strolled up the beach, getting larger and

larger in her vision as he approached, slowly coming into focus until she recognized him.

It was *the man* from the inn. That man who had unsettled her so. What had Susan said his name was? Reed Newman. That was it.

He got closer and her heart skipped a beat. Why did this stranger have such an unexpected effect on her? She drew in another deep breath and forced herself to look at the sea instead of the man slowly approaching her.

She was sure he'd pass by with a brief smile, like nearly all of the beach walkers, each interested in their own journey, their own time on the beach.

As he got close she couldn't help herself, she looked up at him, catching his eye. "Hi." She hadn't meant to say anything, to stop him.

The man paused, staring at her. "Hi. Aren't you the person I ran into on the steps of the inn?"

"Uh, yes. I think we did see each other there."

He stood looking like he was waiting for more.

"I was there meeting my friend Susan. She owns the inn."

"Ah."

Not much of a conversationalist, was he? She pushed her foot into the sand, wondering if it were possible to just slip away into the grains of sand.

"Are you here for very long?" She knew darn well he was here for a month but didn't want to let on that Susan had told her.

"For a bit."

Well, that was noncommittal.

"I should let you get on with your walk." She was running out of things to say to him.

Reed stared at the woman on the beach, the one no longer wearing a stained t-shirt. This t-shirt said *The Sweet Shoppe* on it.

Quit being such a jerk. You know how to talk to women, don't you? What's my problem?

"I, um. Would you care to join me on my walk? I'm just headed to the lighthouse, then back to the inn."

Why had he asked her to join him?

"I could do that. I live near the inn, so I go back that way."

He reached down, and she placed her tiny but strong hand in his. He lifted her effortlessly to her feet.

"I don't know anyone on the island."

Stating the obvious, old boy.

"Well, you know me now. Julie Farmington." She smiled at him.

He realized he was still holding her hand in his. "Newman. Reed Newman."

Julie reached up and grabbed a handful of her thick, chestnut hair, trapping it from the wind's efforts to cover her face in random flyaway locks. "Glad to meet you Newman Reed Newman."

"Sorry, force of habit."

He was a dunce.

He dropped her hand, started walking, and she fell into pace by his side. It was nice to have company on the walk, although he was used to being alone. But this whole vacation thing was so new to him, uneasiness had settled over him. He'd worked long and hard to feel like he was back in control of his life and didn't like the off-kilter way he was feeling here on Belle Island.

"So, did you come to Lighthouse Point to make a wish?" Julie sidestepped a wave coming in and bumped into him. "Oops, sorry."

"No, I'm not much into the make-a-wish thing."

"So you did hear the legend."

"Read about it in a brochure about the island."

"I'm not much into it either, but I do love the beach here. The water is such an amazing shade of azure blues and emerald greens, depending on the lighting."

"I don't blame you, it's beautiful."

They walked on in silence for a few minutes. A sense of comfortable peace drifted around him, one he hadn't felt in a very long time. In fact he could count the exact number of days but he wasn't going to go there. Not now.

"So, what do you do?" Julie's voice interrupted his

35

thoughts.

"Software engineer."

"Oh, sounds interesting."

"It is sometimes. Sometimes it's frustrating."

Like when his boss sends him away from his job for a month.

"Where are you from?"

"Seattle area."

"Wow, you came a long way for a vacation."

"I did. It was a spur of the moment decision. Saw something about the island on TV. Looked nice, so I booked a trip."

"I hope we live up to your expectations."

"So far, so good." He paused at the end of the point. "Should we turn around?"

"Probably. I have things I really should be doing, but I keep wanting to play hooky while I can before the summer crowds take over my life."

"What do you do?"

"I'm a baker. I own The Sweet Shoppe." She pointed to her t-shirt.

"Really? I can hardly heat up leftovers."

"I learned to bake… well, a long time ago. I used to bake for Tally at Magic Cafe. Tally Belle, she's another friend of mine."

"Belle as in Belle Island?"

"One and the same. Her family settled the island. Rumor has it that it was her whatever-amount-of-greats grandmother who made that first wish."

"That's kind of cool to be connected to all that history. Does her family still all live here?"

"Tally is the last of the Belle family line."

"That's too bad."

"It is kind of sad. It will be strange to no longer have a Belle on the island after... well, after Tally is gone. I expect she'll be here for a really long time, though. She's an amazing woman. Like I said, she owns Magic Cafe. She grew it from a tiny stand on the beach to this fabulous restaurant. She did it all by herself. She's just... amazing." Julie grinned.

"Sounds like it. I'll have to try it."

"You should. Try the grouper if you go there. It's the best thing ever."

"I'll do that."

They turned and headed back the way they came. As they walked along, Julie entertained him with stories of the island and tidbits of its history. He had no concept of passing time—which usually only happened when he was engrossed in solving a software glitch—and suddenly they were back at the inn. Julie walked with him to the base of the stairs to the wide, welcoming deck.

"I guess this is your stop." She smiled at him, the expression reaching all the way to her eyes, making them sparkle like emeralds.

"I guess it is." But he didn't want her to go. Didn't want to go back to being alone, a stranger to the town. Before he could think it through he asked, "so, um... would you like to go to Magic Cafe with me tonight?"

She stood on the sand, shifting on her bare feet, seemingly hesitant to answer him.

He immediately gave her an out. "I just thought... you could show it to me. Get some of the grouper. I guess it's really late to be asking though."

"No, I don't have plans." Julie stood and looked at him for a moment. He could still see the hesitation. Of course. She barely knew him.

She turned her head so the wind would blow her hair out her face, looked at him, then nodded. "Yes, I'll go."

"Great." Reed was surprised at the relief he felt about not eating alone again.

"I could meet you there?" Julie asked.

"Sure, that'd be great. Oh, wait, where is it?" Reed sounded like a fool.

"Oh, good call. Tell you what, I'll meet you back here in the lobby at say, six? We'll walk there. It's just down the beach."

"Sounds great." He'd already said that. He could barely get a coherent sentence out around her.

"Okay, I'll see you then." Julie turned and headed down to the water's edge.

He watched her walk down the beach before he climbed the wooden stairs up to the deck. He slowly took each step, feeling off-balanced again. That was silly. He was just going to dinner with a new friend.

CHAPTER 5

Reed stood at the window, again, looking out at the ocean. He felt like he'd spent half his time here on Belle Island staring out at this view. It was the down time, the nothing-to-do time that made him just… stare. He was going to have to find something to do with the hours and days that stretched before him.

At least he'd made plans to go to dinner. He'd been surprised that he'd asked her, it had just slipped out… and words never just slipped out with him.

This was not really a date though. He didn't date. Ever. He'd pretty well perfected the art of seeming unapproachable, and that had served him well. It had been over fifteen years since he'd dated someone new, and he wasn't ready to start now. But it didn't feel like a date, since Julie was coming over here to meet him, then they'd walk to Magic Cafe. Maybe she'd even offer to split the bill. That would make it less date-like.

He sighed because he was fairly certain he'd turn her down if she did offer to pay. So did that make it a date?

No, he didn't date, remember?

He was pretty sure he was losing it, talking to himself, staring out at the ocean for long periods of time. He'd become a crazy man.

He reluctantly pulled himself away from the window and dug through the clothes he'd brought with him. He had casual dress pants, but that almost seemed like overkill for a beach restaurant. He'd come right up to his room after Julie left and looked up Magic Cafe in one of the brochures. It had open-air seating right on the beach, along with another air-conditioned inside section. He'd a hunch Julie would be a sit-outside person.

He grabbed khaki shorts and a clean knit shirt, and in the next moment promised himself he'd go shopping tomorrow. More casual clothes. Sandals. Gym shorts. T-shirts. His face had a touch of sunburn, so he figured he'd pick up a ball cap to wear, too.

He grabbed his trusty brochure to look up the closest places to shop. A couple of clothing stores and lots of souvenir stores were nearby. He could definitely walk to them or ride a bike if he'd get around to renting one. He'd ask Julie where the nearest self-service laundry was, too. He'd need that soon. Or better yet, one where he could drop off his clothes and they'd wash them for him. *Did they even have a place like that on the island?* Back at home, his twice-weekly housekeeper did his laundry. He wasn't sure he even remembered how to do it himself.

He grabbed a quick shower, got dressed in the clothes he'd finally decided on, and headed downstairs to meet Julie.

Julie pushed through the door to the lobby of the inn. She was early, but she was hoping to talk to Susan for a few minutes before Reed came down to meet her. She was pleased to see her friend working the reception desk. Julie waited for Susan to finish registering a couple, then hurried over to talk to her.

"What are you doing here?" Susan looked up from the desk.

"I'm… oh, just shoot me now. I think I have… a… date. Kinda." Julie leaned against the long wooden desk and traced the grain with her finger.

"How can you kinda have a date? Who with?" Susan looked at her expectantly.

"That Reed Newman guy."

"Really?" Susan's eyes widened.

"I saw him again on the beach when I was over at Lighthouse Point. We walked back here and then all of a sudden he asked me to go to Magic Cafe with him tonight. I'd been talking about Tally owning it and… what have I done? I don't even know the man." Julie drummed her fingers on the reception desk. "No, it's kind of crazy, isn't it? I just met him. I mean, I'm just being island friendly, right? Just showing him around."

"Whatever you say." Susan grinned. "I can't remember the last time you had a date. Do you ever date? I mean, really?"

"Same back at you. When is the last time you went out with anyone?"

Susan scrunched her face. "I… don't remember. Who has time for that anyway?"

"This is silly. I don't know why I'm getting so worked up."

"Don't you think you can have a nice time with him? Sit and talk with him at dinner. You know, be a real-live adult person. The kind of person who actually has a life outside of their work."

Julie laughed. "Are there really people like that?"

"I don't know, because since I've hooked up with you and Tally, I've seen no sign of any of us having much of a life outside of our respective businesses. Glad to see you change that trend."

"It's one dinner."

"It's a start." Susan looked past Julie. "Here he comes."

Julie dragged in a deep breath for courage and turned around.

"Hi." Reed walked up and flashed a smile that totally disarmed her.

Julie swallowed. *Swallowed hard.* Then told herself to get it together. "I don't know if you've been formally introduced to Susan." Julie cocked her head towards her friend. "This is Susan Hall. She and Jamie, her son, own the inn."

"I've met them both, but didn't catch their names. Mrs. Hall, nice to formally meet you."

"Please, just call me Susan."

"Susan. Then please, call me Reed."

"Are you ready to go? We can take the sidewalk or the beach. Your choice." Julie caught the wink Susan sent her behind Reed's back.

"Whichever you prefer."

"The beach then, always my first choice."

"You two have a good time." Susan turned to welcome a woman approaching the desk.

Julie led the way out to the deck, wondering what in the world she'd been thinking, saying yes to Reed, an almost stranger. No doubt Tally would be giving her the eye when they got there, too.

Reed had no idea why this woman stole all rational thoughts from his mind. He was a successful businessman. He could tame a computer program like no other. Find errors. Fix them. He was sought after by some of the biggest tech companies on the West Coast, heck in the whole U.S. But this woman reduced him to a stammering idiot.

He decided the better part of valor would be to just... not speak.

So they walked in silence down the beach. He wouldn't call it companionable silence either. Just... silence.

He needed to get over himself. He cleared his throat. "So, ah... how far... is the Magic Cafe?" Well, it was a start at conversation.

"Around that bend." Julie pointed in front of them. "Are you getting tired of walking on the soft sand? It takes some getting used to. It's easier on the packed sand down by the waves, if you don't mind getting a little wet."

"I don't mind." Not that walking on the soft sand was bothering him either, but he'd noticed she liked to walk at the water's edge when she left him earlier today.

They veered towards the water and he gently bumped into her before catching his balance. Okay, sometimes the dry sand *was* harder to walk on. She looked at him and smiled, then they were back to... silence.

He tried again. "So your friend Mrs. Hall, I mean Susan, seems nice."

"She is. But it isn't Mrs. She took back her maiden name after her divorce. Her husband left her. Never met him, it was before she came to the island, but I take it he was a jerk. She helped him grow his business, then he left her for some barely legal-aged woman. Okay, I exaggerated a bit there. But, anyway, she got nothing in the divorce. Nothing. I'm not sure she wanted any of his money… but the thing is, it wasn't just *his* money, because she was a big part of the reason he was so successful. She helped to make that business flourish." Julie stopped abruptly and reached down to scoop up a small shell. She looked at it absentmindedly, then dropped it back to the sand. "I'm sorry. I didn't mean to rant. It's just Susan works so hard, starting all over, trying to make a go with the inn. Doesn't seem fair."

He didn't know what to say to that. It didn't seem fair. But then, he knew better than most that life is not fair. It promised you nothing.

And in his experience, nothing was exactly what you received.

CHAPTER 6

J ulie had no idea what had possessed her to go off like a raving maniac about Susan's ex-husband, a man she'd never even met. For all she knew, Reed had an ex he'd left in the lurch, although somehow she didn't believe that. Her instincts said he was a good man.

They rinsed their feet at the spigot at the edge of the low deck to the cafe and slipped on their shoes. Tally looked up and crossed over to greet them. "Hey, Julie. I didn't know you were coming tonight."

"I was tired of cooking. I brought my… friend… Reed."

"Always glad to have a new customer. Nice to meet you, Reed. I'm Tally."

"Good to meet you."

"I have a table at the edge of the sand, would you like that? Or do you want inside?" Tally looked at

47

Reed as if she were sizing him up, an outside diner or inside one.

Julie looked up into Reed's sky-blue eyes and forgot what she was going to ask for a moment. *What was it? Oh, yes.* "Is outside okay for you?"

"Fine by me."

Tally led them to a table and handed a menu to Reed. "I'll send someone for your order. Can I get some drinks for you?"

"I'll have a beer." Julie sat in her chair and looked over at Reed.

"Tea for me."

"If you order tea down here, it will be sweet tea, is that okay with you?" Julie always gave *foreigners* a heads up. She remembered how surprised she'd been when she moved down here and ordered tea. After a while she'd gotten used to the sweetness, and regular tea tasted funny to her now.

"Sure. That's fine." He sat down and picked up the menu. "No menu for you?"

"I have the thing memorized. Though nine out of ten times I get the grouper. The only decision is blackened, fried, or baked with lemon sauce."

They ordered their meal and sat and sipped their drinks.

"The cafe is interesting. Never saw a restaurant that flows right onto the sand."

"Yep, my favorite tables are the ones out here on

the edge. I've already kicked off my sandals and I'm digging my feet in the sand." Julie grinned at Reed.

"Tally is doing a good business for off-season, isn't she?"

"Tally does a fairly good business all year round. In the winter if it turns cold, she has roll-down sides for the deck and some ceiling heaters. This is a favorite of locals and tourists. You'll love it, trust me."

"I'm sure I will." Reed leaned back in his chair and looked out at the ocean. "Nice view."

"Just wait until sunset. It looks like with those clouds out there we might get quite a show tonight."

Reed turned his attention back to her. "So, a baker. How did you learn to bake?"

Julie bit her lip and looked away for a moment, always hating to talk about her past. "I... well, I lived in this one foster home for about a year. The grandmother lived next door. She was great. She taught me to bake. Pies, breads, fancy desserts, muffins, you name it." She shifted and looked away for a moment. "Then... I had to leave."

"You grew up in the foster system?"

"From eight until the day I turned eighteen."

"To be honest, I've never known anyone who grew up in foster care. Did you move around a lot?" Reed stopped and peered at her. "Or are my questions too personal?"

As a rule, Julie never talked about living in foster care, but for some reason she didn't mind talking to

Reed about it. Well, at least talking about part of it. There were some things about living in foster care she'd never told anyone, and she never planned to. "I did move a lot. I think I had a total of about fifteen placements. Some group homes, some foster parents. The longest I was ever in one place was a year."

"That has to be rough."

Reed's eyes were filled with pity, the exact thing she didn't want from him.

"I learned to be independent, had that great year where I learned to bake—which made it possible for me to have my dream now, my own bakery. So, it's all good." She probably wasn't fooling him. It honestly *had* been horrible growing up. New homes, getting lost in the shuffle, new schools and always, always, struggling to fit in. Something she'd never quite accomplished. Hoping against hope she wouldn't be sent away yet again.

Luckily their meals were delivered and Julie moved the subject to the grouper and hush puppies.

Reed carried on a conversation about the food when Julie changed the subject from her past, but his mind churned around Julie's comments about growing up in foster care. His parents were gone now, but he'd grown up in an honest to goodness white picket-fence home with family dinners most nights. Okay, the home had been more like an estate, but still. He'd been an only child and attention had been showered on him. Maybe that's why the solitude hit him so hard now.

But look at all Julie had gone through. He wanted to ask what had happened to her parents, but he could tell she'd been eager to change the subject, so he kept up his half of the fish and hush puppy conversation.

When the bill came Julie reached for it. "Here, I've got it. Island friendly and all that."

"No, let me get it. It was nice to have someone to talk to during my meal." That very thought startled him. It had been nice. He was so used to eating alone, he'd forgotten how pleasant chatty dinner conversation could be. At least they'd gotten past the awkward silence.

He paid the bill, they said goodbye to Tally, and headed out onto the beach.

The evening darkened, and just as Julie had promised, the sky burst into orange and pink flames, wrapping around the thunderhead clouds out over the ocean. He'd never seen a sunset quite as spectacular.

Julie sank to the sand at the edge of the beach, and he sat beside her. This time their silence was in awe of the magnificent painting nature sprawled across their view. He could feel the heat of her arm as it brushed against him. Julie randomly scooped up handfuls of sand and let the grains sift through her fingers as she sat watching the sunset.

"It's so breathtaking, isn't it?" Julie's voice was low, filled with wonder.

"It is one of the most remarkable sunsets I've ever seen." Not that he stopped to watch sunsets —like ever.

The ocean lit up with the reflected colors, like watercolor splashed across the waves. They sat quietly as the evening sky darkened and random stars began twinkling in the night.

"We should probably head back before it gets too dark to see. Although I sometimes walk the beach at night when there's a full moon. It's all so peaceful then." Julie stood and brushed the sand from her shorts.

He stood beside her, mimicking her motions and swiping the sand from his clothes, too. They walked the few steps to the water's edge, of course. By now he knew this was Julie's trail of choice. As they walked back towards the inn, they fell into an easy rhythm of matching steps. He couldn't remember the last time he'd felt so at ease and comfortable with someone. Well, he knew exactly how long it had been... and that thought burst his mood into a million shards of pain.

Julie didn't know what happened, but she could feel Reed pull away and distance himself from her. Not in actual inches, but it was like his mind pulled away. They continued down the beach until she couldn't stand it any longer.

"Are you okay?" She stopped and tugged gently on his arm to stop him. "You seem… distant now."

"I just… sorry. It's not you. It's me. I'm a horrible date, I guess. I mean if this is even a date." Reed raked his hand through his hair. "I'm just not used to… this."

"If it makes you feel better, Susan said she couldn't remember the last time I had a date. You know, if this is a date." Julie grinned up at him. She was pleased to see the side of his mouth crook into a smile.

"Yep, let's call it a date. We'll have bragging rights and can mark our calendars that we've finally had one," Reed teased.

"Perfect. I'll let Susan and Tally know so they can quit bugging me to go out. Not that either one of those two has time for dating either."

"Well, a person has to eat, don't they? We could do this again. You know, sometime when you have to eat."

"I eat every single day." The corners of Julie's mouth twitched into a smile.

"That makes it easier on us, doesn't it?" Reed started walking and Julie fell into step beside him.

As they got close to the inn, Reed turned to her.

"Can I walk you home? I hate for you to walk on by yourself."

"You don't have to do that."

"I'd like to, though. It's the way my mom raised me." Reed looked shocked. "I'm sorry, is that a rude thing to say to you? I know your parents didn't raise you."

"You're allowed to have parents. Good ones, even." Julie tugged his hand. "Then we'll cut through here if we're going to my house. It's just up this road."

She led him up the side road and crossed over to her street. Should she invite him in? Did she want to? She wasn't quite ready for the night to end, but she was at a loss on this whole dating thing. She climbed the steps to her front door and turned to him. "I had a good time."

"I did, too. A really nice time."

Ask him in.

No, maybe I shouldn't..

Ask him.

Before she could finish her argument with herself, Reed stepped away and onto the sidewalk. "I'll see you soon, then. Goodnight."

"Goodnight." Julie turned and unlocked her door.

Foolish woman, you should have asked him in.

CHAPTER 7

Susan made sure she was waiting at the kitchen door to the inn when Julie arrived with her deliveries the next morning. "How was your date, not date?"

Julie handed her a tray of baked goods. "It was fine."

"Fine. That's what I'm getting? Come on, help a friend out. Give me some details. Let me live vicariously through you."

"Okay, it was really nice. I think we're going to go out again." Julie paused. "Though we didn't set anything up. I wonder if he was just saying that."

"Tally called last night after you left Magic Cafe. She said it looked like you two were having a good time."

"So you're talking about me behind my back?"

Julie grinned and grabbed another tray, this one loaded with pies.

"Of course. We always talk about you. What are friends for?"

Julie walked into the kitchen and Susan pressed a cup of coffee in her hand. "Here, give me five minutes."

Julie glanced at her watch, then took a sip of the coffee. "Okay, five minutes. Then I have to run. I have the new worker starting today."

"So did you find out what he does?"

"Some kind of computer geek, I think." Julie crinkled her forehead. "We actually talked more about me than him."

"Tell me it isn't so. That never happens." Susan sipped her coffee as she leaned against the steel counters in the immaculate kitchen. That was one thing she was a stickler about. Absolutely everything was ship shape in the inn's kitchen, even if most of it was outdated and worn.

"I know. He was just kind of easy to talk to. We talked and walked. Oh, hey, did you see that sunset last night? Wasn't it fabulous?"

"I did. Jamie came and dragged me out to the deck to watch it. It was gorgeous." Susan cocked her head. "So, do I get any more details?"

"He walked me to my cottage."

"Did you ask him in?"

"By the time I finished arguing with myself about

whether I should, he'd already walked away." Julie shrugged. "Don't know if that's good or bad. It might have been nice to sit up on the widow's walk and talk a bit more."

"Well, if you do go out and he does walk you home again…" Susan paused and gave Julie her best don't-mess-with-me look. "Decide in advance to ask him in."

"I should clean my cottage, shouldn't I?" Julie laughed.

"Might be a good idea." Susan pushed away from the counter and reached for Julie's cup. "I'll let you go now."

"You're going to call Tally as soon as I leave, aren't you?" Julie raised her eyebrows and laughed.

"You betcha."

Reed decided he could kick himself for not going ahead and setting up another date with Julie. Why hadn't he just asked her out again last night? He'd left in such a hurry because he hadn't known whether he should stay or leave. He tilted his head from side to side, loosening the muscles. He must have been tense last night on the date, because today his neck and shoulders were screaming at him. He reached a hand up and massaged the muscles.

He walked over to the small desk in his room and

poured himself another cup of coffee, trying to decide if he wanted to go downstairs for the breakfast buffet or take a walk first. He was reluctant to admit it, but he was beginning to enjoy this beach walk thing. He never had time in his hectic life in Seattle to just relax and take a walk. Or relax and do anything. He always pushed himself to stay busy. It helped him forget…

He shook his head, unwilling to start down the path of feeling sorry for himself. He glanced over at the stack of brochures on the desk. He absentmindedly flipped through one of them until he saw an ad for The Sweet Shoppe. That was Julie's place.

In a burst of decision he set down his coffee cup and headed to get dressed and go to The Sweet Shop. He'd ride the bike he'd finally gotten around to renting yesterday. If Julie was at the shop, he'd ask her out again. Another plan, a bit of purpose to his day. It beat standing in front of the coffee pot rifling through island brochures.

Within twenty minutes he was pushing through the front door of The Sweet Shoppe. A bell jangled above him. It was mid-morning, and most of the tables were filled. The bakery was painted a cheery yellow. It stopped him in his tracks. It seemed like the island was determined to throw the color in his face. He'd noticed last night that Julie's house was painted a creamy yellow color, too. A color he studiously avoided when at all possible.

A young woman motioned to him to take an empty table near the window. He looked around, purposely ignoring the golden walls, but saw no sign of Julie. A wave of disappointment swept through him, which he quickly stomped down. No use being silly about the woman. He'd gone out with her once. If it took a while to connect with her again, it was no big deal. Not at big deal at all.

He glanced around the shop and saw the large chalkboard over the display cabinet. The specials of the day were listed. Peach muffins. Cinnamon rolls. Raspberry croissants. They all sounded tempting. The waitress came by, poured him a cup of coffee, and took his order for a peach muffin. "Want to look at today's paper?"

Reed nodded and took the paper from the waitress. It was the Sarasota paper. He glanced through the headlines, realizing he hadn't been keeping up with the news at all. Usually he was a watch the news, read the news, news alerts on his phone kind of guy. This week at the island he'd gone all off the grid as far as news went. He liked that. He folded the paper and decided there was nothing in it he needed to know.

He looked up and Julie was heading his way with a plate, an enticing-looking muffin balanced on it. "Hi, there." Her smile lit up her eyes.

"I decided to come see your shop."

"Glad you did. You picked a good choice. Peach

muffins are one of my favorites." Julie set his plate in front of him. "I've got to go in the back and help out with some baking, but I'll be back to check on you."

He wanted to say something to make her stay, to persuade her to sit and chat with him while he ate. But instead, he watched her walk away. He ate the very delicious peach muffin, wishing he'd ordered two of them. The waitress came back and asked if he wanted anything else, but he figured it would be wrong to say yes he did, he wanted Julie to come back out and chat with him. So instead, he shook his head no and she dropped his check on the table.

He stalled as long as he could, sipping on coffee, but Julie didn't come back. He should have asked her out while he had the chance when she'd dropped by the table. He kept missing his opportunity.

He stood up to pay his bill. He fished some money out of his pocket, left the tip on the table, and headed to pay at the register. The waitress rung him up and handed him his change. "Oh, and Julie said for you to go on back to the kitchen and see her."

So, all this time he'd been dawdling, and all he had to do was check out to learn she wanted to talk to him. The waitress nodded towards the kitchen, and he pushed through the swinging doors. The kitchen was bigger than he'd imagined, filled with stainless counters, two sizable sinks, a large industrial-looking dishwashing station and some huge ovens. It was also intensely hot.

Julie looked up from behind a counter. Flour dusted one of her flushed cheeks, and she shoved a lock of hair away from her face with the back of her wrist. "There you are. See that tray over there? Go try one of those. A new recipe I'm working on."

Reed spied the tray of delicious-looking something or others, dusted with powdered sugar. Ah, maybe the white layer on Julie's face was sugar, not flour. He refrained from reaching out to swipe a finger across her cheek to taste the white powder to find out.

"They're almond scones."

He tried one, and it was amazing. Melt-in-his-mouth amazing. "Wow, this is great."

"Thanks. I tweaked the dough recipe a bit. I think it turned out nicely."

"It sure did." He eyed the tray.

Julie laughed. "Go ahead, have another one."

He took her up on her offer and watched as she made up another batch of the scones. "Do you do all the baking?"

"I used to, but now I have another baker, thank goodness. She's in the back room right now."

He watched her hands as she worked with the dough, added ingredients, all the while talking to him about her business. He was a bit in awe of her efficiency. She put a tray of scones in the oven and turned to him. "I've set the timer on my phone. Want to go out back while they're baking? I need to get out of this hot kitchen for a few minutes."

"I'd like that. I'm beginning to melt in here."

"We have air conditioning units, but one of them is acting up this week. Need to get it looked at before it turns any hotter. There's always something begging for a slice of my profits." She walked over to a large refrigerator, reached inside, and grabbed a large pitcher of water. "Want some?"

"Sure do."

She filled two large glasses and led him out back. Outside the door was a small oasis. A large tree provide shade over a small brick patio. A wrought-iron table and chairs were at one end of the patio, and a glider was placed across the other end. Julie sank onto the glider. He didn't know whether he should grab a chair at the table or sit beside her. He was such a man of indecision when he was around her. Where was the self-confidence that surrounded him in the business world?

Julie patted the glider. "Come sit."

He lowered himself beside her, careful to give her enough room. She pushed her hair away from her face and rubbed a hand across her cheek, leaving a trail in the dust of white on her cheek.

Julie looked at the back of her hand and saw the powdered sugar. She must look a mess. Her cheeks were flushed—she could feel their heat—and her hair was in damp ringlets around her face. She put the cold glass up to her cheek in an effort to cool off. She really need to get the air conditioner fixed, sooner rather than later.

She'd been so happy to see Reed sitting at the table when she'd peeked out into the shop today. Very happy. It was a feeling that totally threw her, in an out-of-control kind of way, and she never liked to feel out of control. Not anymore. She'd had too many years of others deciding her future and making decisions for her. Now she carefully made every decision and directed her own destiny.

But this man put her on edge. Not really in a bad way, but different than she'd ever felt. Off-kilter. Like she was running at full speed down the beach not knowing what she was running towards.

"I'm going to go shopping this afternoon." Reed took a sip of his water. A lone bead of condensation from the glass dropped onto his shirt. "I need some... well, play clothes, I guess. Sandals. T-shirts. Casual shorts. I don't know what I was thinking when I was packing to come here."

"Oh, there's Island Closet, a great shop for casual clothes. And there's the Wishing Shop. It's souvenirs and t-shirts and stuff like that."

"That sounds good. I'll have to find out where they are. Can I walk there?"

"You can basically walk anywhere on the island, but there's also the trolley you can take. If you want to wait until after The Sweet Shoppe closes at two, I'll go with you and show you where they are."

What was she doing? She was asking him out. Though showing him the shops wasn't a date.

"That sounds great. I need to find a laundry, too."

"You could use my washer and dryer. Why don't you come over for dinner tonight? You can do your laundry while we eat."

He was going to think she was a crazy woman, asking him to do things with her all the time.

"I hate for you to cook for me. You spend all morning in the kitchen."

"It won't be anything fancy. Maybe we could grill something?"

"How about we stop by the market and pick up the makings for dinner after our shopping spree? At least let me buy the groceries if you're going to all the trouble to shop with me and cook me dinner."

"It's a deal. I'll pick you up at the inn about two-thirty. I'll drive, so we can haul your laundry over and get the groceries. Plus, how do I know you're not a big-time shopper and you might buy more than we can carry home?" She grinned at him.

"I can't remember the last time I shopped. I usually order things online."

"This will be a rare treat for you, then." She winked at him and glanced at her phone. "I've got to go in and grab those scones out of the oven. I'll see you this afternoon?"

"Yes. I'll be waiting."

Reed stood on the front porch of the inn. The paddle fans on the ceiling stirred the afternoon heat, and it was actually quite pleasant out on the porch. Julie pulled up in a van that said *The Sweet Shoppe* on the side in large swirling letters. The van had seen better days, he could tell that.

He climbed into the van and dropped his bag of laundry behind the seat. "I'm ready. I think."

She grinned at him. "I promise I'll make it as painless as possible."

"I'd appreciate that."

"Shopping isn't that scary, really."

"If you say so."

He couldn't remember when he'd last gone shopping for any kind of clothes. His wife, Victoria, had taken care of that for him. She'd always said she was a better shopper and he was horrible at choosing what went with what. A pang raced through him.

Now was not the time.

He pasted on a smile as Julie pulled away from the inn.

They wandered through Island Closet. Julie pointed out the most comfortable brand of sandals, so he snagged a pair in his size. He found some casual shorts to add to his to-buy pile.

"No, put that baseball cap back. Try this." Julie handed him a straw hat. "It'll keep the sun off your face and be cooler than that cap."

He tried it on. It fit but…

"Perfect." Julie smiled. She snatched it off his head and punched it up a bit. "Much better."

She found a Hawaiian-print shirt with palm trees and parrots and handed it to him.

"Really?" He looked at the shirt skeptically.

"Really. Trust me. This brand is made from a breathable fabric. You'll love it."

"If you say so." Reed really couldn't imagine himself in it, but what the heck. Julie was having so much fun picking out things for him.

They headed to the Wishing Shop for t-shirts. Here Julie was in her element, choosing shirts with abandon.

"I love t-shirts." Julie grinned. "Wear them every day at The Sweet Shoppe."

"I've noticed."

"You really need at least one Belle Island t-shirt."

"I'm sure I do."

Julie picked out a bright yellow one.

"Not that one." Reed panicked a bit. "I don't do yellow."

"Okay, how about this one with the lighthouse on it? Make a wish at Lighthouse Point. You want to support our foolish folklore, don't you?"

"Sure…" Reed wasn't a sayings kind of t-shirt guy,

but this one wasn't yellow and he'd quit second guessing Julie's choices over an hour ago. Well, except for yellow. Never yellow.

They grabbed their bags of purchases and Julie drove them back to her cottage.

"Here, bring in your new clothes and we'll wash them before you wear them."

"Oh, we don't have to."

"Yes, we do. Gets the sizing out of them."

Reed never washed the items he ordered online before he wore them the first time, but he didn't think it was worth the argument. Julie seemed fairly determined in her stance. He liked that about her… *mostly*. "Okay, you win. We'll wash all of this."

They carted his laundry and the bags of new clothes into her cottage. Julie quickly sorted them into piles and threw in the first load.

"The grocery store is just around the corner. We could check the fish market, too. Might have a good catch of the day we could grill. Do you want to just walk there?"

"Sounds good." Reed was really getting into this walk-to-everything lifestyle.

They found some snapper and picked up salad makings at the market. They walked back to the cottage and switched out the laundry, then Reed headed outside to start the coals. Julie had a small backyard with a couple of palm trees in the corner. A patio held a white wrought-iron table and four chairs with an umbrella poking up through the middle of the table. He started the barbecue and popped up the umbrella to give them some shade.

Julie pushed through the backdoor with two tall glasses filled with clinking ice. "Hope you like lemonade."

"Haven't had any in years, but it sounds really good." He reached for a glass. "The coals should be ready in a bit."

They sat at the table in the shade of the umbrella.

Julie propped her feet up on an extra chair. "So, Seattle. Do you like living there?"

"I do, I guess. I've lived there for years." He watched, entranced, while Julie put the cool glass up to her face.

"Where did you grow up?"

"I, uh." He pulled his attention from the glass against Julie's rosy cheek. "I grew up in the Midwest. Kansas City."

"Really? I lived in Illinois. We were almost neighbors." She smiled. "What brought you to Seattle?"

That question. The one he didn't want to answer. He sat for a moment while she stared at him. "I, um… my wife got a job out there, so we moved."

Julie's eyes widened.

"Your wife?" Julie narrowed her eyes, looked at his bare ring finger, then searched his face. He hadn't been acting like a married man, and she sure as all get out wouldn't be hanging around with one. "Divorced?"

"Ah, no." He looked out into her yard, took a sip of his lemonade, then set the glass on the table. "She's... gone. Passed away a few years ago."

"I'm sorry." Julie felt guilty for her momentary distrust of him.

"You know, I hate all the terms for death. Passed away. Sounds like someone just walked into the sunset. Died. Such a short word and so harsh. Another one I hate—lost one's life—like someone would lose their keys or their wallet." He turned and stared at the palm trees.

"I guess I never really thought about all the ways we say someone is... gone." There, now he had her second guessing her choice of words.

Reed cleared this throat. "I should check those coals."

The pain was palpable, an aura of grief surrounded Reed. She connected with him in some strange way, the sense of loss. She knew that feeling. Not of death really, but of loss, of being left behind.

Julie wondered how his wife had died, but could see Reed had closed the subject. She got up from the table. "I'll bring out the fish."

"Thanks." Reed still poked around at the coals, avoiding looking at her.

She brought him the fish to grill then went back inside, threw in another load of laundry, and made the salad. She poked her head out the door. "Hey, do you want a beer with dinner?"

"No, I'll stick with lemonade."

"Okay."

She brought out a tray with plates, a pitcher of lemonade, and the salad. They ate outside on her table. The rest of the evening was strained though, and Reed often looked lost in thought. After their meal, Reed helped her clear the table and bring the dishes inside.

"Thanks for letting me do my laundry here."

"Any time. Why don't you fold that last load while I do the dishes? I left a laundry basket by the dryer. You can take the clothes back to the inn in the basket. I'll get it from you later."

Reed nodded and headed to the laundry room. Julie stood at the sink, mindlessly rinsing the dishes. She'd seen the deep pain in his eyes when he'd mentioned his wife, the kind of searing pain of loss that burned to your soul. She knew that kind of loss only too well. But she'd had years to help dull the pain. His loss was more recent and obviously still raw.

Reed came back in as she was finishing the dishes. "I think I'm all set now. Thanks again for the loan of the washer and dryer."

"You want to go up to the widow's walk and watch the sunset? It's got a great view."

"Maybe next time."

Julie's heart squeezed in her chest. Turned down. That hurt. But she could see him struggling ever since he'd told her about the death of his wife.

"Fine, I'll take you back to the inn now." She grabbed the keys to the van.

"Thank you."

Their stilted conversation hung in the air, and she mourned the easy way they'd teased each other when they'd been out shopping. Which made her think of the term "mourn your loss," which then just drove her crazy. Was she going to analyze every expression relating to death?

She climbed into the van and slammed the door with a bit more force than was necessary.

CHAPTER 8

Tally and Susan entered The Sweet Shoppe the next morning. Julie looked up and smiled at her friends. Susan had that determined look Julie recognized so well.

"Grab that table in the corner. I'll bring coffee over for you."

She grabbed some heavy ceramic mugs, poured them both black coffee, and went to sit for a few minutes.

"So, I heard you were seen in town with Reed yesterday." Susan nailed her with a tell-me-everything look.

"And when I went to the fish market, they said you'd been in there with some strange guy yesterday," Tally added.

"He's not that strange…" A smile tugged at the corners of Julie's mouth.

"Spill it." Susan wasn't taking any dodging of questions.

"Yes, I took him to Island Closet and the Wishing Shop. He needed some more casual beach clothes. We cooked dinner at my place and he did his laundry there."

"And?" Tally raised one eyebrow.

"And… things were great until they weren't." Julie sighed. "We had a good time. Then I found out he was married."

"He's married?" Susan put down her coffee mug with a clatter.

"No, he *was* married. His wife… passed away." She was never going to know the right term to use for dead, ever again.

"That's too bad. Recently?" Tally's face was etched in knowing empathy.

"A while ago. A few years, I think. He's obviously still haunted by it. Anyway, the discussion put a damper on the rest of the evening. He didn't say much when I dropped him off at the inn. Didn't say anything about seeing me again. I didn't want to be the one to ask him to do something after he… cooled off towards me. I'll wait and see if he asks me out again."

"He'd be a fool not to." Susan laced her hands around her mug.

"He's fun to be around. Awkward sometimes, but

honestly, I don't know if that's him or that's me. It's not like I'm an experienced dater or anything."

"Well, not since Troy." She sighed. Troy. He'd been one big long two-year mistake. He'd dated her and hinted at commitment and marriage. Then, just when she'd started to trust he really did want to be with her, he'd left with barely a comment as to why. She never should have let her guard down with him. She knew better.

"It's been, what? Five years?"

"Susan, give the girl a break. If she doesn't want to date, then she doesn't have to." Tally sent Julie a questioning glance.

"It's not that I don't want to date—and Susan, you're one to talk—but I rarely have any free time. And we all saw what a lousy choice I made last time. I think since Reed is so… fragile right now. I can call a guy fragile can't I?" Julie sighed. "I'm better off just taking a wide berth around him, right?"

"If you never want to know love. True love." Tally bent her head and stared into her coffee cup, obviously lost in long ago memories.

Not that the three of them ever talked about Tally's past. Julie knew the gist of it, but none of the specifics. She just knew Tally had great loss in her life, too. They all had.

Susan set her coffee mug on the table and looked directly at Julie. "I'm not a great judge of character, as evidenced by my ex-husband. But I wouldn't have traded a minute I had with Jamie's dad, not even to avoid all the pain when he died. Love like that is rare. But if you don't ever take a risk, you'll never get a chance at a really good, strong love. The soul mate kind of love. That kind of love… that's something you don't want to miss out on."

"Do you really believe in soul mates?" Julie cocked her head.

"*I* do." Tally's low voice drifted across the table like a rose petal in the wind, a hint of wistful sadness wrapped around her words.

Julie's friends left The Sweet Shoppe, and she went back to waiting on customers. She didn't know what she was going to do about Reed. Probably nothing, because he'd shown no interest in asking her out again.

"Julie. There you are. How *great* to see you."

Julie spun around at the sound of that voice. "Ah, Camille."

What the heck was Camille Montgomery doing here? Her family lived in a big, rambling house directly on the beach. Well, not exactly lived in it. More like popped in for a bit here and there. In the winter to escape the cold. In the summer for a vacation. Camille actually lived up north in some small town in Mississippi. Julie wasn't usually so judgmental, but Camille rubbed her the wrong way.

"Mama asked me to come down and meet with the interior decorator. We're redoing some of the furnishings. The beach house was just beginning to look so *tired*. We want it all spruced up. Mama is throwing a big party next weekend. You know, before the ghastly summer tourists swarm the island."

Julie was pretty sure Camille's tired furnishings were better than anything she had in her own cottage. And while Camille wasn't exactly a tourist, she wasn't exactly a regular resident either. She'd met Camille years ago when Julie had worked at Tally's. Camille had come in regularly, carefree and laughing, always with a bevy of other girls her age. Not a one of them had any responsibility for anything but perfecting their suntans. They'd treated her like their personal servant, without a please or thank you ever given.

"Julie? Are you listening?" Camille's voice pulled her from her memories. "Mama said I should talk to you and see if you were capable of handling some of the appetizers and desserts for her party. I told her I just wasn't sure if your little shop was up to it. I know we could always get someone from Sarasota to handle it. We have a caterer doing the dinner, but their appetizer and dessert offerings—I just got back from sampling them—well, they aren't up to Mama's standards. But then she suggested you…"

Yep, there was the Camille that got on her nerves.

"I'd be happy to talk to you or her about what

you'd need." Julie wasn't foolish enough to turn away good business, even if it meant working with Camille.

"Are you sure? Mama is having over a hundred people. She's booked rooms at the inn as well as using our guest house and main house. And it is *next* weekend."

Susan hadn't said anything about that. Oh, maybe that was the fully booked weekend Jamie had mentioned.

"When is it exactly?"

"Next Saturday. Are you sure you can handle it? It will be a pretty big order for you, I bet."

Julie gritted her teeth. "I've handled baking for events as large as four hundred people, Camille."

"Oh, well then. I guess you'll do."

Sometimes, Julie wondered if Camille was for real.

"I have to run to the Sarasota airport and get Delbert. Delbert Hamilton of the Hamilton Hotels, you've heard of them, of course?"

It was more a statement than a question.

"We've been dating for quite a while. He's taking a few days off and I want to show him around. He'll be back again for Mama's party, of course."

"Of course."

"I'll try to run by here tomorrow with Mama's list of suggestions for what she'd like for the party. Of course, cost is no object for Mama. You're sure you can handle it on such short notice?"

"Yes, I'm sure. What time will you be by?"

"Oh, I don't know. I have so much to do. But sometime tomorrow."

I'll just sit and wait around all day for you...

"I better hurry. Don't want to keep Delbert waiting." Camille spun around and headed out the door in a flounce of southern belle entitlement and way too much perfume.

Julie sank into an empty chair. She could use the business, but she didn't relish the thought of working with Camille or her mother. She shoved a wayward lock of hair away from her face. What had she just gotten herself into?

Reed walked to Lighthouse Point and back, not even trying to deny he was hoping to run into Julie. He wanted to apologize for his... *weirdness* last night. He'd gotten quiet and distanced himself, he knew that. It was just such an easy role for him to drop into these days. A role he felt comfortable with. A role that had served him well the last few years. But he'd seen that look in Julie's eyes last night. Confusion. Distrust. He couldn't blame her.

Unfortunately, he had no luck spotting Julie. He rinsed his feet at the showerhead by the steps to the inn and climbed the stairs, one by one. Each step taking him closer to... what? He could go up and sit in his room and stare out at the ocean again. He had no purpose. No direction. What the heck did people *do* on vacation? He'd already caught up on the top journals and websites in his field. He'd almost logged into the company server to grab some files and deal with some loose ends of projects he'd been working on before he left, but he figured his boss had his login flagged to notify him if there was any activity. His boss had been serious about Reed taking a break.

He walked inside and ran into Mrs. Hall. Miss Hall. Susan.

"Hello, Reed. Coming in from a walk?"

Was he imagining it, or was Susan's tone a bit less friendly now? She'd probably already talked to Julie, who had probably already clued her in on what a jerk he'd been last night.

"Yes, I went to Lighthouse Point and back."

"Oh, out there making a wish?"

"No, no wish. Just the walk."

"A nice day for it. Well, I need to head to the kitchen and talk to the cook." Susan turned away and hurried down the hall.

He climbed the stairs to the top floor. The elevator still had a sign proclaiming it was out of order, though he'd seen a man working on it before he'd left on his walk.

Reed entered his room and dropped his key on the dresser. His laptop bag sat on the desk, mocking him.

Then it came to him. He could work on the

smartphone app he'd had rambling around in his mind for the last year or so and see if he could make it work. He grabbed his leather bag—*the one Victoria had given him*—and pulled out his laptop. He sat on the bed, leaning back against the mound of pillows.

Victoria had loved having mounds of pillows on the bed, on the couch…

Don't go there…

He flipped open his laptop, determined to get lost in his project. For the first time since his boss had banished him, he started to feel alive again. He opened a file and started making notes of all his ideas for the app.

When he looked up again, he was amazed to see it was evening. His stomach was rumbling, and he snapped the laptop shut. He moved his shoulders forwards and backwards, trying to loosen the stiffness.

He grabbed his wallet and the key to room—a real key with a diamond-shaped plastic tag with the room number printed on it—and headed out the door. With no clear plan in mind, he decided to wander to Oak Street. He'd seen in his trusty brochures—they were getting crinkled and worn from countless times of opening then carefully refolding them—that Oak Street had a string of restaurants and shops, along with an impressive live oak tree and gazebo at the end of the street. He'd have dinner at the first place that caught his eye.

CHAPTER 9

Julie pushed through the door to The Lucky Duck. She was in no mood to cook, and a grilled burger and the best fries in town sounded like just what she needed. A cold beer to chase it down wouldn't be so bad either.

She stood inside the door, giving her eyes a moment to adjust to the darkness. Misty Hartman was in the corner, tuning her guitar and getting ready for a set. That was a fortuitous coincidence. She loved Misty's music. The night kept looking better.

"Hey, Jules." Jamie waved from the far end of the bar.

Jamie always called her Jules. He had since they'd first met when he was in Belle Island one summer working for his uncle at the inn. The inn he and his mother now owned since his uncle's death.

"Hey, Jamie." She slipped onto a barstool beside him.

Willie Layton, the bartender, came up behind the bar. "What'll you have?"

"Cold beer. Burger and fries."

"Instead of your regular beer, you wanna try my new drink?" Willie swiped the bar clean in front of her.

"What's that?

"A basil-motonic."

"What is *that*?"

"You should try it, it's really great." Jamie pointed to a tall glass in front of him.

"It's kind of a cross between a mojito and a vodka tonic." Willie cocked an eyebrow.

"Sure, I'll try it."

"Great. It's going to be our new signature drink here at The Lucky Duck."

Julie thought a draft beer was more their signature, but didn't want to belabor the point.

"You look like you've been hit with a truck, Jules." Jamie dipped one of his fries in ketchup and munched on it.

"Why thank you. That's so nice of you to say." Julie rolled her eyes.

"She does look a bit peaked, doesn't she?" Willie joined in.

"*Peaked?* Gosh, boys. Be careful. You don't want to make a girl feel special or anything."

Willie plopped a tall glass in front of her and she wasted no time taking her first sip. "Ah. That's really good, Willie. The day just got better."

"I don't suppose your mood has anything to do with Camille? Mom said she was back in town. Camille's mother actually booked every empty room at the inn next weekend."

Julie took another sip of the —what had Willie called it? Basil-motonic? "And, lucky me. I'm catering some of her party. Desserts and I'm not sure what. Camille wants me to sit around all day tomorrow waiting for her to drop by and discuss."

"Which you will do." Willie winked.

She sighed. "I will. Because I could use the business. Besides, it's good promo for me to do more events like this. You never know who will be there and might hire me for some event they are having themselves."

A couple of younger women, dressed in impossibly short shorts, walked into the bar.

"I should wait on them." Willie grinned.

"I'm sure you should, buddy." Jamie nodded soberly, then winked.

Julie just shook her head. Willie never missed a chance to flirt with a pretty woman.

"I heard you went out with the Reed guy who's staying with us." Jamie offered up his fries while Julie waited for hers.

She reached over and took one. "I'm pretty sure there are no secrets in this town."

"No, I'm pretty sure there aren't. So do you like the guy?"

"Did your mother tell you to ask me that if you saw me?"

Jamie grinned. "Possibly."

"Look, I just spent a little time with him. It was not big deal. Really. Why do people keep asking me about him?"

An alarmed look settled on Jamie's face, he cocked his head, and almost imperceptibly shook his head no.

"What? It was nothing. He showed no interest in me other than my shopping knowledge, and the fact I own a washer and dryer. The big-city guy's not interested in me."

"I'm sorry you thought that."

Julie spun around at the sound of Reed's voice. "I. Um…"

"I apologize. I wasn't at my best last night. I do appreciate the loan of your washer and dryer. I'll find a Laundromat for the rest of my stay." Reed spun around and headed towards the door.

"Nice one, Jules." Jamie dunked another fry while Julie shot him a look of exasperation and jumped off the stool.

"Reed, wait." She reached out and grabbed his arm. He paused and turned towards her. "Do you want to join Jamie and me at the bar? I just ordered.

They have great burgers here. I'm sorry about what I said. You just… Honestly, Reed. I don't know where I stand with you. You run hot and cold and I hate not knowing when I'm going to say the wrong thing." She looked at him and squared her shoulders.

He looked at her a long minute, his deep blue eyes searching her face. "Fair enough. Let's start over." He reached out his hand. "Newman. Reed Newman."

She grinned at him and placed her hand in his. "Farmington. Julie Farmington." She tilted her head towards where she'd been sitting. "Now, will you join us?"

"I will."

They walked to the end of the bar and Reed took the barstool beside Julie's.

Willie delivered her dinner and looked at Reed. "What can I get you?"

"I'll have what she's having. Though make my drink a soda."

"You sure? It's my famous basil-motonic."

"Sounds fascinating, but I'll stick with soda."

"Coming up." Willie placed the order and went back to chat with the short-shorts at the end of the bar. Both were flirting outrageously with Willie, and he was enjoying every minute of it.

~

"You know Jamie, right?" Julie perched on a barstool in between the two men.

"Yes, I met him at the inn." Reed nodded at Jamie.

"And the bartender is Willie. See, you're getting to know quite a lot of people on the island."

"I am, thanks to you."

"You out exploring the island tonight?" Jamie took a sip of his drink.

To be honest, the drink sounded interesting, but he hadn't had alcohol since Victoria died. He hated the thought of it, the smell of it, the look of it. He pulled his thoughts away from the basil-motonic. "I just decided to head out and have dinner at the first place that caught my eye."

"So was it the huge carved parrot outside, or the bright neon sign that pulled you in?" Willie placed the soda on the counter.

"I actually saw on the outside display board that there's live music tonight."

"That would be Misty." Julie nodded towards a young woman of about twenty-ish, setting up in the corner on a small raised stage.

"We get a lot of the local talent in here performing." Willie turned and headed over to the ledge between the bar and the kitchen. He grabbed a couple of plates and walked down to where two young women were sitting sipping on his basil-motonics, by the look of it. Reed watched the trio for a moment, a bit envious of the easy repartee going on among them. When had he ever been that easy-going or carefree? He could hardly remember what it was like.

"So are you enjoying your vacation?" Jamie interrupted his thoughts.

"To be honest, I don't really do vacations well. I'm not much of a just sit around and do nothing person. I've walked your beaches and stared at the waves. Poked around a bit on Oak Street. But I'm not sure what to do with all my time. Well, I wasn't until today. I started working on a personal project. A smartphone app. Been wanting to try my hand at that for a long time, but never carved out the time to actually work on it. Started it today. I actually had a really good time working on it."

"And that's vacation to you?" Julie cocked her head.

"Well, yes. I really enjoy it. Programming it. Designing it for ease of use. Making the app sync between phone and computer. It's a challenge and I'm learning something new."

"I'm not much for just sitting around either, so I get that." Julie looked at him. "At least you can enjoy the ocean view while you're working on your app thingie."

"It does feel good to have a… I don't know… a purpose to my time off."

"I would just like to have some downtime. Can't think of the last time I had even a few days off." Jamie pushed away from the counter. "You know, I should encourage Mom to take some time off. Go visit her sister. She hasn't had a break in forever, either." He glanced at his watch. "And I really need to get back to the inn. See you two around."

Willie brought the burger and fries, and Reed and Julie sat and occasionally made comments, but mostly just ate and people watched. It wasn't the healthiest meal he'd ever eaten, but it was really good.

"May I walk you home?" Reed looked at Julie, wondering if she'd blow him off, or whether he'd made amends enough that they could still be friends.

Or whatever they were.

"I think I'm going to stay here a bit and listen to Misty sing."

She didn't ask him to join her.

"Okay, then. I'll see you later."

Julie nodded.

Reed dropped some bills on the counter to pay for his meal and headed out the door, disappointed in how the night had turned out. He should have asked her out for a date later this week, that's what he should have done. He stood outside the door to The Lucky Duck and deliberated whether he should just go back inside and ask her. He let out a long breath of air. He was horrible at relationships, dating, or even friendship, for that matter.

～

Julie sat on the barstool and sipped on her basil-motonic. At least she was getting used to Reed's hot and cold, friendly and distant attitude.

"Julie."

She spun around at the sound of Reed's voice.

"Do you mind if I sit with you and listen to Misty sing? And I thought maybe you'd like to go out with me tomorrow night?"

Well, she wasn't expecting that.

"Yes, sit. Misty is really good."

He sat next to her. "And the date tomorrow?"

She smiled at him. "That would be nice, too."

Misty played a set with a mix of folk and country songs. When it was over, Julie stood up. "I should be going. It's always an early day for me."

"Will you let me walk you home?" Reed stood up.

Julie looked at him for a moment, unsure of her answer, unsure about so much. Should she let him walk her home? Should she ask him in when they got there?

Reed stood, his hand on the counter as if trying to decide if he should sit back down, silently waiting for her answer.

"Sure, I'd like the company." There, a decision was made. He could walk her home. They headed towards the door and Willie winked, then grinned at her. She rolled her eyes at him as they walked passed.

Reed raised an arm and pushed the door open for her. She slipped out into the warm night air. The outside tables were filled with customers enjoying the late spring evening. They headed down Oak Street towards her cottage. A golf cart passed them on the street and she waved to her first-of-the-morning customer, Dan Smith. "See you in the morning, Dan."

"Hoping for blueberry." Dan waved.

Julie leaned her head, nodding towards the disappearing golf cart. "That's Dan. He's always the first one in The Sweet Shoppe in the mornings."

"I noticed quite a few golf carts on the roads here. I'm guessing that's allowed?"

"Yep. You'll see a lot of them, especially in the winter when the snowbirds—the winter tourists, the ones who spend the winter—are here. They seem to like their golf carts to get around. A few of the bigger rental places have larger golf carts for the renters to use. Susan keeps talking about getting some that her visitors could rent while they are staying at the inn. I think it's a great idea, but it adds up. Buying the carts, batteries, maintenance, repairs. She keeps wavering."

"It probably would be a headache to keep up with all of that."

"There are a few cart rental places on the island. Though honestly, a lot of people just walk or take the trolley."

"The trolley is the tram-like thing I've seen going by?"

"Yep, they add on more sections to it during the busy season to hold more people."

They fell into step on the sidewalk as she led him towards her home, still undecided about asking him in. Why, oh why, was she making it into such a big deal?

Because of Troy. That's why, and she knew it. She wasn't really ready to trust another guy, and Reed had been so hot and cold with her, she didn't trust him. There. Her mind was made up. She'd just send him on his merry way.

They walked up to her door and she was plenty pleased with herself for having made a decision.

"So, does that offer to see the view from the widow's walk still stand?" Reed looked at her.

She bit her lip and sighed inwardly. So much for decisions. "Sure, why not?"

Didn't that sound enthusiastic?

"I usually take a glass of wine up there with me. You want one?"

"No, I don't think so. Thanks, though."

He must not be a drinker. She'd never seen him have any alcohol, ever. "I still have some lemonade."

"I'd like that."

They went in and she made a tray with a pitcher of lemonade and two glasses. He took it from her as they climbed the narrow spiral stairway to the widow's walk. The room at the top was small, with just her comfortable chair

93

and an end table. She opened the door to the walkway outside. A cool breeze blew in from the coast.

"This is nice." Reed set the tray on the small table she had outside.

They sat on the two chairs she had out on the walkway. She pointed to the bay and the lights twinkling far across on the mainland.

"This is really a great spot." Reed sipped his lemonade.

"It is. I spend so much of my time at home up here. Either out on the walkway, or in the little room."

"I see you have the room equipped with a nice over-stuffed chair."

"I had to get a friend drive a truck into the backyard, and we put a ladder up from his truck bed to the outside of the widow walk. We brought the chair in from the outside. I was determined to have that chair up here."

"I guess you were."

"I like to read up here, and that is my favorite reading chair."

"What kind of books do you read?"

"Romances, mostly. Happy ending books. An occasional mystery. Sometimes whatever book is hot right now, just to know what people are talking about. Do you read much?"

"Only about computer stuff. I used to read

thrillers, but… well, I just don't have time and don't think about reading anymore."

"You should pick up a book to read on your vacation."

He furrowed his brow. "You know, I should."

"Shopping and reading. Wonder what I'll have you doing next?" She grinned at him.

~

What would she have him doing next?

She seemed to push him out of his comfort zone, which he wasn't really sure was where he wanted to be. Not at all.

He wasn't used to staring at a woman's face, waiting for her to break into a smile. He wasn't used to the easy way they could talk—when he wasn't screwing that up. He wasn't used to hoping she'd say yes to going out with him…

"So, where do you want to go on our date tomorrow? You're the island expert. Dinner? Movie? Or?" He looked over at Julie, her face dimly lit from the moon that kept hiding behind clouds then shyly peeking out before ducking for cover again.

"Honestly, I usually do Magic Cafe or The Lucky Duck. There is a fancy place here… I've never actually been there. Three Wishes."

"So is everything on Belle Island named after wishes or luck or magic?"

"Pretty much." She grinned at him. "The Wishing Shop, A Wish and a Player—get it—it's a sports bar. Or they are lighthouse this or that. Lighthouse Gift Shop. Names like that. We love our tourist trade and play into it with gusto."

"I guess you do."

"But seriously, our tourist trade is what keeps this island alive. We depend on it. You either work on something in the tourist trade, or fishing. That's ninety percent of the jobs on the island."

"Aren't you afraid a hurricane will wipe you out?"

"It's hurricanes here on the gulf, tornados in the Midwest, earthquakes or wildfires in other places. There is always a threat of a natural disaster. We don't go borrowing trouble, we just go on with our lives, day by day."

"Not a bad philosophy." That's really how he lived his life now, too. He didn't look to the future, he just moved through each day.

Julie stretched out her legs. "I don't mean I *don't* look to the future."

He stared at her, her words were so similar to his thoughts. Well, actually, the exact opposite of what he'd been thinking.

"I'm always planning. I have ideas to expand. Maybe open another shop in Sarasota, or maybe in another beach town. I'd like to get the catering side of the business to grow." She shrugged. "I have big dreams."

He looked at Julie, her eyes shining with hopes and plans. Had he ever been like that? So excited about the future? So full of hope and dreams? Belief that the future would be all bright and rosy?

"Don't you have dreams? Things you want out of your future?" She raised her head and looked directly at him.

"I... don't. I don't think about the future much now. Everything... changed... when Victoria died. She took my plans and my dreams and my future with her."

Julie looked at him silently for a moment, then touched his hand. "I didn't know your wife, but do you think she would want you to just shut down? To stop living? You've been given a life and it seems so wasteful to just... throw it away."

"You don't understand what it's like."

"Maybe I don't. I've lost a lot in my life, but not a spouse. But you don't have to let that one loss define you, define your life. I've tried to move on from mine."

"Maybe you're a stronger person than I am." He'd no doubt she was. She'd had a tough life and she'd overcome it. He just couldn't seem to move past the accident.

But then, he didn't deserve to move on because the accident had been all his fault.

CHAPTER 10

The next morning Reed carried his laptop down to the lobby and saw Jamie working the front desk. "Hey, Jamie. I can't get my laptop to connect to the internet."

A wry grimace spread across Jamie's face. "Yes, that. The internet is down. Again. I have a guy coming out to look at it in an hour or so. But that's on repairman island time, so who knows when he'll actually make it here."

"You know somewhere else I can go and grab some free wireless?" Reed wanted to search for help on the internet. He was stuck on programming his app.

"The Sweet Shoppe has it. Jules' internet is usually better than ours. Unless the whole island is down. That happens. Often."

"I guess I'll go try there, then." Reed stepped out into the humid, late-morning air that offered no breeze to chase away the mugginess. He put his laptop in the basket of his bike, rode the short distance to the bakery and slipped inside, glad to be out of the oppressive heat. If it was this hot in April, what was it like here in August? Well, he wouldn't be around to find out. He was ticking off the days until he could return to work in Seattle.

Except then he saw Julie behind the counter waiting on a customer, and he wasn't quite so eager to get back home.

Julie waved from across the room, and he crossed to an empty table near the wall, after glancing around to find a power outlet if he needed it for the laptop. He settled into his chair and popped the laptop open. No internet signal here, either.

Julie walked up. "If you're looking for internet, I think it's down island-wide."

He sighed. "I was. Jamie said you might have access. Trying to get some work done and needed to search for some info."

"I thought you were on vacation."

"This is personal work, not work-work."

"You're out of luck unless you want to drive over to the mainland."

That sure wasn't going to work for him, now was it?

"I guess I'll just wait for it to come back on."

"Good plan." She shrugged. "It's island life. We're pretty laid back about all things techie. Makes it a bit harder to run a business, though we've all learned to deal with the occasional outages."

"I guess I'll have to eat my frustrations away." He grinned at her, pleased to see an answering smile in return. "You got any of that almond goodness you were making the other day?"

"I do. Two almond scones and coffee?"

"Perfect."

She delivered his breakfast, and he worked on his app for a bit, still wishing he could hit the internet to help him figure out where he was going wrong on his programming. The door to the bakery opened and a large crowd of young teens dressed in softball uniforms and a handful of adults came into the shop.

He looked over at Julie, who had a hint of a deer-in-the-headlights look in her eyes. She motioned for them to take seats anywhere and hurried into the back, probably looking for reinforcements.

With a quick moment of decision, he pushed back from his table, walked over to the sideboard, and grabbed a tray of glasses and a pitcher of water. He walked up to the first table of giggling girls and plopped down glasses of water for each of them, then continued until every single one of those young, laughing schoolgirls had water.

The noise level grew to a volume unknown to him. Noise, laughter, giggles… and a crash. He turned to look at a broken glass at a nearby table.

"I'm sorry." A blonde girl in braids looked stricken.

"Not a problem. I'll just get something to clean that up. Be careful of the glass."

Julie came out from the kitchen and shot him a surprised but thankful look.

"Broom and mop? And I'll get that cleaned up for you."

"You don't have to do that."

"The broom?"

"In the kitchen, just ask Nancy."

He cleaned up the mess, then came back out and watched as Julie moved efficiently from table to table, taking orders. He grabbed the coffeepot, eager to help, and walked around filling coffee mugs for the mothers who accompanied the girls.

Julie brushed past him. "You don't have to do that either... but thank you. The new girl I hired is moving into her apartment today, so it's just Nancy and me."

"No problem. What else can I do?"

"I'll grab the orders and tray them up, and you can deliver them to the tables?"

"I can do that."

He spent the next hour helping Julie, delivering orders, filling glasses, refilling mugs. The girls and their mothers finally left for their softball tournament and Julie sank into a chair at the only clean table in the bakery.

Reed sat beside her. "Well, that was certainly an experience."

"I really appreciate your help. We rarely get big groups like that. I usually look at the island website though, and check to see if there are going to be tournaments around here. But, well, the internet is down, isn't it?" Julie looked at him and laughed. "You look exhausted."

"I am a bit. Who knew that many young girls could be so... loud?" He rolled his shoulders.

"And hungry." She grinned. "That's the important part. I'll say that was a good morning of business."

The door opened and they both turned to look. A man dressed in a nice suit stepped inside with an impeccably dressed woman on his arm.

"There you are, Julie. Did you just have that whole crowd of girls we just passed on the sidewalk in here?" The woman glanced around the bakery with a look of distaste clearly plastered on her perfectly made-up face. "I came over to discuss Mama's catering order with you, but look at this mess."

Reed saw Julie bristle at the remark, but just as quickly her face broke into a businesslike how-can-I-help-you look. He stood up and offered his chair to the woman. "I'll clear the tables while you talk to... I didn't catch your name?"

The woman smiled at him and flipped her hair off her shoulder. "I'm Camille Montgomery. And this is Delbert. Delbert Hamilton of Hamilton hotels."

Reed had heard of the chain of luxury hotels but wasn't sure why that was part the man's introduction. "Nice to meet both of you. I'll just get out of your way and let you talk to Julie."

The woman drummed her paid-for-a-manicure fingers on the table. "I don't know, Julie. If you can't handle a group of girls, do you think you can manage Mama's order? Mama will be crushed if everything isn't just perfect." The woman dramatically brushed away invisible crumbs and gingerly slipped into the chair Reed had vacated.

"It will be perfect. You just tell me what you want."

Reed began to clear the nearest table, and Julie shot him a thankful look.

Julie closed the door behind Camille and looked at the notes she'd taken. It was going to be a big order, and she knew everything had to be perfect. It would be good for her business to get her name out to the people Camille's mother would be inviting. Other owners of big houses here on the island. A few business owners from Sarasota. A handful of out-of-town guests, but who knew if they'd fall in love with the island and come back and rent one of the homes here. She always was looking to make connections and expand her business.

She walked into the kitchen and found Reed at the dishwashing station, rinsing the dishes. "Reed, really. You've done enough. Step away and let me finish those up."

He backed away from the sink, splattered with water and flushed from the heat of the kitchen.

"Look at you. I'm so sorry."

"It was interesting. Haven't waited a table since my first year of college, but I think I did okay."

"More than okay. You saved me."

"Everything go okay with that Camille woman?"

"As well as anything goes with her." Julie sighed. "I've got to make sure everything goes right with their order. I'm going to go all out on this job. I'm doing desserts, a large cake, and some appetizers. She has someone else bringing the main meal. Prime rib, I believe she said."

"Sounds like a big order."

"It is." Julie looked at Reed. "Would you mind if I cancelled out on tonight? I really want to sit down and plan out this order and see what vendors I need to contact to make sure I have everything I need."

"You have to eat." Reed's face was covered in disappointment.

"Have you noticed I work in a bakery? I never go hungry." She grinned at him.

"I guess that's true."

"I don't have time to go out for a fancy dinner. But you could come here if you'd like. After we close this afternoon, I'm going to try out some new appetizer recipes I might use for Camille's party. If you don't mind a mix of appetizers for dinner… and a pastry for dessert, you could come here for dinner."

"I'd like that."

"Perfect. Why don't you come around six o'clock? Come to the back door and I'll have it unlocked."

"I'll see you then." Reed turned and headed out to the front, probably glad to escape the heat of the kitchen.

Julie walked over to her small desk in the far corner of the kitchen. She sank into a chair and started scribbling down ideas before the lunch crowd hit.

Reed showed up promptly at six o'clock with a bouquet of flowers he'd bought from Flossie's Flower Shop. He'd picked a mix of brightly-colored flowers, careful to avoid anything yellow. He rapped on the frame of the open back door. A huge fan blew across the kitchen, and he could tell Julie hadn't heard him over the roar of the fan. He watched her for a few moments as she pushed back a lock of hair with the back of her wrist, a simple motion he had come to expect from her while she was engrossed in her baking. She stood mixing something in a stainless steel bowl in front of her. She looked up and waved a flour-covered hand, motioning him to come in.

"These are for you." He held out the flowers.

She raised her dough-covered hands. "Thank you. They're so pretty. Could you put them in that pitcher over there for me? I'm just finishing up this last batch, then I'll grab us some food and we'll go sit outside. It's got to be cooler out there on the patio than in here."

"Still haven't gotten the air conditioner fixed?"

"I'm calling the repair guy tomorrow. I can't take it any longer. I'm hoping it doesn't cost a fortune to fix it. It keeps cutting out."

"Want me to look at it?"

"You know air conditioner stuff?"

"Just a bit. Let me at least look at the thermostat and see what I can figure out."

"Tool box is in that storage room." Julie pointed to a door on the far wall.

He grabbed the tool box and pulled the cover off the thermostat. He checked the wiring and found a loose wire. He fixed that then placed the cover back on the thermostat. "Let's try this."

The compressor kicked on and soon cool air poured into the kitchen.

"How'd you do that?" Julie pushed back a damp lock of hair.

"Magic. Isn't this island about magic and wishes?" Reed winked.

"Well, you made that wish come true for me."

"And you didn't even have to walk out to Lighthouse Point." He placed the tools back into the toolbox and returned it to the storage room.

Julie covered the bowl of dough, put it in the refrigerator, and set out a tray of appetizers she had snagged from the oven. "Grab that tea, will you?" She nodded at a pitcher and two glasses sitting on the counter. They went outside and sat in the shade on the patio.

"This is so much nicer. I hope the kitchen cools off soon. Nancy will be so pleased to find the air conditioner working again."

"My father taught me if your air conditioner is acting strange, always check the thermostat first."

"Good to know. Not that I'd know what I was looking for."

"Just a loose wire connection."

"I'll have to have you show me how to do that. I like to know how to fix things myself."

He'd already figured that one out. She was an amazing, independent woman who had come a long way with her life and created a successful business from nothing. He admired her hard work and dedication.

"You're staring at me." Julie looked across the table at him, pausing mid-bite on a tantalizing appetizer.

"I'm sorry." But he wasn't really. He liked watching her, listening to her… just being with her.

But the next second guilt crashed over him. What

right did he have to feel like this, sitting here and enjoying a meal with another woman? Like nothing had happened. Like it hadn't been all his fault Victoria was gone. His pulse pounded in his temples and his breathing quickened.

He stood up, knocking over his chair in the process. "I... can't. I just can't."

She looked at him for a moment and nodded. "Okay. I understand." She paused for a moment. "But, Reed? Don't come back around again. I can't do this, either. Not like this. Not this off and on with you."

She picked up their plates and headed inside.

He ran his fingers through his hair, torn with indecision. Eventually the guilt won out, and he turned and walked slowly away. Away from any chance with Julie. Away from her friendship and laughter. Away from that look of distrust and disappointment in her emerald-green eyes that probably would haunt him the rest of his life.

Reed wandered aimlessly down the road, threading his way towards the beach through a haphazard maze of side streets. When he reached the beach, he looked both directions. He could return to the inn or walk on the beach and try to sort out his jangled nerves.

He caught a glimpse of the lighthouse in the

distance and resolutely headed that direction. He walked along, step by step, along the water's edge. He passed a few others out strolling, each time giving a perfunctory smile, then walking on silently. The breeze off the sea tousled his hair, reminding him he hadn't found a place on the island to get his haircut yet.

But then maybe he should just leave the island. He was pretty sure Julie would be glad to see him go. He couldn't blame her.

He was a mess. He knew that. He just didn't know how to fix himself, to rise above the guilt and move on. But did he even deserve to do that? If only he'd listened to Victoria that night and not insisted he get his way. But it was too late to change that, and too late to save her.

Too late. Too late. The words reverberated in his mind with each step he took. He finally reached Lighthouse Point and sank onto the sand, staring at the ocean.

Julie had been right the other day when she said Victoria wouldn't have wanted him to throw his life away like this. He knew that, and yet… he couldn't forgive himself.

He looked up and down the beach and saw not one person. Feeling a bit sheepish, he pushed himself up and crossed to the edge of the sea. A lone, perfect shell called to him. It was a pale shade of orangey-yellow.

Yellow. That figured.

He leaned over to pick it up, allowing a gentle wave to wash the sand from it. He stood staring at the shell in his hand for long moments of indecision. He tightened his fist around the shell and looked out into the ocean.

I wish you could forgive me, Victoria. I wish I knew how to live without you.

Before he could stop himself, he threw the lone shell into the sea.

Not that he believed in the legend.

Not that he thought it would do any good.

The sky burst into a million shades of pink and yellow as the sun slipped below the horizon. He spun around when he swore he felt someone's hand on his shoulder, but no one was there. He was alone. Always alone. He turned and headed back to the inn, finally admitting to himself something had to change. He couldn't go on like this.

CHAPTER 11

Julie gave up on sleep, climbed out of bed early the next morning, and headed to the bakery. She had the deliveries packed up and ready to go thirty minutes ahead of schedule. She decided to drive over to the inn. Susan was bound to be up, she was an early riser just like Julie and Tally.

She pulled the van up to the kitchen entrance to the inn and slid out of the van. Susan came out, took one look at her and pulled her inside. "What's the matter? You look terrible."

"Gee, thanks." Julie took the offered cup of coffee.

"No, really. What's wrong?"

"It's Reed. Just when I thought we were making progress and I relaxed my guard a bit, he turned all cold on me and walked away. Said he couldn't do it. Whatever *it* was. I'm not sure what we were, but I did like spending time with him. He made me laugh, he treated me like he respected me, admired me even. But I cannot take his wavering. I just can't. I told him not to come back around. Not that I think he will. He made it quite clear he isn't ready for a relationship. Not that we even had a *relationship.*"

"I'm sorry, hon. First guy I've seen you have any interest in, well, forever. Now this."

"He has some kind of survivor guilt thing going on with his wife's death. I get that. But then, why does he come around? Why does he act like he wants to be with me then it's just... poof, gone, outta there, running away?"

"Well, it's probably better now than later, before things went any further with you two."

"Probably." Julie set down the coffee and reached up to rub her shoulder. The tense muscles refused to relax as she kneaded them. "Anyway, I need to just move on. I was up half the night over-analyzing everything I said to him. What made him finally run away."

"You know it's not you, right? It's him. Something he'll have to learn to deal with. Or not."

Julie sighed. "I suppose so. I keep thinking I said something wrong or did something wrong."

"Seriously, Julie, cut it out. Everyone deals with grief in their own way. He obviously hasn't dealt with his. He needs to before he can move on with someone else."

"I know that in my head, but my heart still stings a bit from the rejection."

Susan wrapped an arm around Julie's shoulder. "I'm sorry."

"So am I." Julie pulled away. "I just need to go back to work and forget him. I have the catering of Camille's mother's party next weekend. I have so much to do. Keeping busy will be good for me."

"Ah, yes. Mrs. Montgomery's party. We have an inn full of their guests next weekend. Not that I'm complaining. Being full during the off-season is great. Though I did get a phone call from Camille demanding fresh flowers in all the rooms along with a small snack basket in each and every guest room. I quoted her a darn fair price for that and she said she'd get back to me. We'll see. I'll need to contact Flossie's Flower Shop soon if I'm going to need that many arrangements."

Julie grinned. "Camille will probably call you the day before."

"And add something else she wants." Susan shook her head. "I'm going to call her today and say I better darn well hear from her by tomorrow if she wants the flowers and baskets." Susan grinned. "Only I'll say it nicer."

"Good luck with that." Julie set down her coffee. "I better get the rest of my deliveries finished. Then I need to finalize the order for the Montgomery's party."

"Maybe we could meet for drinks one night this week before the rush of the weekend?"

"Maybe. Let me see how far I get on things."

"Just let me know."

Julie went out to the van and brought in Susan's daily delivery, then headed back outside. She climbed into the van, noticing she still hadn't done anything about the rip in the van seat. Just one more thing to deal with. Or not.

Susan worried about her friend. Julie didn't open up to many people, she didn't trust easily. Now this Reed fella had done a number on her. She understood loss as well as the next person. She still ached for Jamie's father after all these years. But a person had to pick up the pieces and move on.

Julie had experienced so many losses in her life, too. Her parents. Getting kicked around from foster home to foster home. Julie rarely talked about her childhood, but Susan knew that time of her life had molded her into the slow-to-trust person she was today. Then there was the whole Troy fiasco. All those promises, then he just up and left. But something between Julie and Reed had just clicked. Julie had decided to try with Reed.

Julie *had* let her defenses down around Reed for some reason, even though she knew he was a shaky prospect. But then maybe she'd wanted to help Reed. Maybe Julie could relate to the loss and the ache in him.

Susan shook her head. Maybe she should go back to getting breakfast ready for the morning instead of over-analyzing her friend.

Fifteen minutes later her cell phone rang and she dug it out of her pocket.

"Did you see Julie this morning? She's not looking good. I'm worried about her."

Ah, Tally had seen Julie, too.

"I did see her. Talked to her a bit. That Reed guy should just leave her alone. No more of this flakey nonsense."

"I agree. And if you see him today, you should probably tell him to back off." Tally's voice had a crisp edge to it.

"I hate to drive off a month-long customer, but I do feel like giving him a piece of my mind."

"I'm going to make up a reason to drop by the bakery later today and see how Julie's doing."

Susan laughed. "She'll know you're checking up on her."

"I'm sure she will, but that's what friends do."

Susan tapped off her phone and slid it back in her pocket. Tally was right. Friends do make sure their friends are doing okay. They'd just have to keep a close eye on Julie for a bit and try to cheer her up. For about the millionth time in her life, Susan gave thanks for her friendship with Tally and Julie. She would do anything for either one of them.

~

Reed opened his leather bag and reached in for his laptop. The laptop caught on the worn fabric lining. He probably should consider getting a new bag, but couldn't bear to do that. Victoria had given it to him on their very first Christmas together. He'd used it every day since then. Victoria used to slip little notes into the bag and sometimes he'd find them at work. They always made him smile.

He emptied his papers and a few pens out of the bag to take a closer look at the lining. He fingered the material and decided he'd take the bag to a repair shop and get a new lining put in. That way he could continue to use the bag for years. The leather was soft and worn from the years of use, but it still held up well in a battered leather kind of way.

He turned the bag upside down and a few paperclips and receipts fell onto the table. He reached for the scraps of paper and his breath caught in his chest. A yellow slip of paper.

Victoria's handwriting.

He reached out and slowly and carefully smoothed the page. He looked away for a moment, his legs seemingly unable to hold him anymore. He sank into the chair, frozen in time, getting ready to read a note from Victoria like he'd done so many times before.

The room sucked the air right out of him and it took all his strength to open that one small slip of paper.

Hi Boo,

He paused then and closed his eyes. Boo, her pet name for him.

I hope you know how much I love you, how much happiness being married to you has brought me. I hope you are happy too, because that's all I've ever wanted... for you to be happy.

You'll have my heart forever, no matter what.

But enough mushy stuff, I still think you cheated at cards last night. I should have won, admit it.

She put a big smilie face after that sentence and he could hear her teasing voice.

Don't forget to bring home some ice cream.

Love,
Sunshine

Sunshine. His nickname for her. Not only because yellow was her favorite color, but because she was that person, the one in the perpetual good mood, who always looked at things as glass half full.

He wondered if he'd remembered to bring home ice cream that night...

Reed pressed the note to his heart while wave after wave of emotion rolled over him, like the surging tide outside his window.

He didn't know how long he sat there. He reached up and touched the dampness on his cheeks, the first tears he'd shed since the night of the accident when he'd held her in his arms and begged her not to leave him.

He got up and walked over to stand by the window. Again. Looking out at the sea. The sea had become a tonic for him, a soothing, healing balm for his soul. The sound of the surf, the mesmerizing march of the waves always headed to shore, never ending.

Victoria's words ran through his mind, over and over.

That's all I've ever wanted... for you to be happy. For

you to be happy. Happy.

He walked out onto the balcony letting the sea air, the warm sun, the surf noise, and the sparkling waves do their magic. For the first time in a very long time, he began to feel. He could feel the pain, but he could also feel the love. It was like he was beginning to thaw after a long, long winter.

An old man walked along the shore, reached down to pick up a shell, and dropped it into a small pail he carried with him.

A shell.

The shell.

The one he'd thrown into the ocean at Lighthouse Point, asking for Victoria's forgiveness and a way to get on with his life. Could the legend be true? Did he get his wish with finding the note from Victoria?

That's all I've ever wanted... for you to be happy.

A peace he hadn't felt in years flooded through him. He could go on. It's what she wanted. Suddenly his senses heightened. The taste of the salt air, the brush of the breeze against his skin, the sight of the sunlight dancing across the waves. For the first time in a long time, he had hope.

He turned around, determined to go find Julie. Talk to her. If she'd even listen to him now. He couldn't blame her if she just tossed him out, but he was going to try and convince her to give him one more chance. Just one more. He wouldn't disappoint her this time.

CHAPTER 12

R eed tromped down the stairs of the inn—the elevator was still out of commission—and paused for a moment, undecided whether to take the roads or the beach. All he knew was he was going to go find Julie, talk to her, and try to explain himself. Beg her, if necessary, to give him just one more chance. He was sure he had his mind all sorted out now. Sure of it.

"Mr. Newman."

Reed turned to see Susan standing beside the landing.

"I thought we'd agreed on Reed and Susan." He smiled at Julie's friend. Any friend of Julie's was a friend of his. Heck, the way he felt now, everyone was a friend of his.

"I wanted to talk to you for a moment." Susan

ignored his remark about being on a first-name basis now.

"Sure, what's up?"

"I should say this is none of my business… but, well, it is my business. Julie is my business. You've hurt her. For some unknown reason she's a bit taken with you."

"She likes me?" Reed felt his heart soar.

"She does. Did." Susan sighed. "You've acted like her friend, she let you get close to her, then walked away. She's not in a place where she can handle that."

"I know. I was just… a jerk. I was trying to sort it all out. I'm okay now. Really I am. I've made peace with my past."

"That's good. I'm glad you have. But that doesn't make any difference. Julie has walled herself off now. I can't blame her. You need to stay away from her."

"But I was just going over to talk to her. To explain…" Reed shifted from foot to foot.

"It would be better if you just let the whole thing drop." Susan pinned him with a look just like his mother used to throw at him when he'd done something wrong. "You're going to be leaving soon anyway. There is just no point, is there?"

"No point?"

"Say you talk to her and get friendly again. Where does it lead? She still ends up getting hurt when you return to Seattle. I know she seems like this strong, independent woman—and she is—but under all of that she is still this lost little girl afraid of rejection, afraid of being left behind."

Reed stood without moving, letting Susan's words sink in. She was right. He was leaving. What did he have to offer Julie except a week or so of friendship, then he would head back to his world and leave her on Belle Island. Julie wasn't really the type looking to be someone's vacation fling. Not that he wanted a fling…

He grudgingly agreed with Susan. "I see your point."

"So you'll leave her alone?"

"That's probably for the best." A swish of emptiness whirled around him. He thought he had things figured out, but he'd only been thinking of himself, not Julie. Not what was best for her. She'd had people leave her over and over, and that was exactly what he would do when he headed back home.

"Yes, it's the best thing for Julie." Susan's eyes were filled with sympathy for him, but edged with protectiveness for her friend.

He couldn't find the voice to answer her, so he simply nodded in agreement.

"I hope you'll continue your stay with us. You are more than welcome, but I understand if you feel the need to leave." Susan turned away and headed back into the lobby.

Reed was certain the offer to continue his stay was

said to be polite, not because Susan meant it. He rested a hand on the stair railing, not knowing if he should go up and pack his things or stay for the rest of his vacation. He couldn't decide. Stay here and not see Julie? It just didn't seem... right.

Someone pushed through the door from the deck and the bright sunlight streamed in, beckoning him. He'd take a walk on the beach while he decided what to do and let the ocean cast its magic.

Julie couldn't decide what was worse. Should she stay at the bakery and keep silly busy so she wouldn't think about Reed, or get out of here before Nancy tossed her out? Julie had dropped a bowl of dough, burned a batch of croissants, and spilled a pitcher of tea.

"Julie, why don't you go take a walk? Clear your head. You're obviously upset about something." Nancy wiped up the last of Julie's mishaps.

"I should stay. There's so much to do. I really need to finalize what we're making for Camille's mother's party." Tension twisted through her. The responsibility of the bakery and the party. The feeling of rejection from Reed. The lack of sleep last night. All of that piled onto her shoulders with a weight that was impossible to dislodge.

Nancy reached out her hand. "Leave the list of

what you're thinking of making with me. I'll check our supplies after the bakery closes. When you come back later, we'll finalize things, okay?"

Julie hated to bail, but she knew she was no good for anything right now. She'd do what Nancy suggested and take a walk, giving herself a chance to settle her mind and her nerves. She gave Nancy a quick hug. "Thanks. I'll get out of your hair. I'll be back soon and in a better mood, I promise."

Nancy shooed her away with a dish towel and headed to the counter to put in yet another batch of almond croissants.

Julie took off her apron and hung it by the door. She pushed out into the sunshine and took a deep breath of the salty air. Yes, this was just what she needed.

She headed to the beach, slipping off her shoes as soon as she got to the sand. She wandered down the beach towards Lighthouse Point, the place that never failed her, the spot where she could always sort out her thoughts.

Julie walked on, the afternoon sea breeze drying her tears as they slipped down her cheeks. She didn't really know why she was crying. Not really. She'd just met the man about a week ago, right? So why did she feel so empty without him? That was just... silly.

She dashed away the last of the tears. She never cried, and didn't know why this man had the ability to reduce her to a weeping fool, but she was finished with that. Julie continued down the beach and made her way to the point. She picked up a lone shell, then dropped it onto the sand. She was not going to be sucked into the silliness of Lighthouse Point.

The sun ducked under the gathering clouds and the wind picked up, chasing away the earlier humidity. Out at sea, she could see a storm beginning to make its way to shore.

She sighed and turned back towards town, she was well aware of how quickly storms could come racing onto shore. The beach was mostly clear of walkers now that the weather was turning from beautiful sunshine to dark gray, ominous clouds. She walked on, refusing to think about Reed.

One step, then the next. Away. Away. She was walking away from any and all memories of him.

A sharp pain in her foot jolted her back to reality. She stumbled and splashed into the ocean, soaking herself. She sat up, still surrounded by the shallow waves. Her heel burned in the saltwater. She raised her leg and looked closely. Blooded flowed from a cut on her heel.

Could the day get any better? She stood up and hopped on one foot until she could sit down in the dry sand, not that it mattered since she was dripping water.

She'd better call Tally or Susan to come get her. She reached for her phone in her back pocket and pulled it out. It was dead, of course. It had drowned in a watery grave of seawater when she fell.

She looked down the beach and it was empty. Everyone had hurried to get inside before the storm hit.

Reed headed down the beach. He wasn't sure if he passed many people or not, because he'd given up the customary quick smile and nod after the first person he passed. He watched his newly tanned feet and the occasional wave that rushed over them and walked on, lost in thought.

Susan was right, of course. He'd no business trying to start up anything with Julie. How could she possibly be interested in a man who was leaving in a few weeks? After what Susan had told him about Julie being afraid of people leaving, how could he do that exact same thing? It wasn't fair to her. Maybe Susan was right and he should just leave the island and head back west.

Make a decision, man.

A rumble of thunder in the distance called to him and he looked out across the sea. Big thunderheads rose above the horizon. He glanced towards Lighthouse Point and figured he could make it there and back before the storm. It might be nice to walk and watch the storm roll into shore anyway.

He continued down the beach, lost in his thoughts. The way Julie made him feel. Actually *feel*, after all these years. The way her chestnut brown hair danced in the breeze. Memories of Julie's quick smile, her laugh, the sound of her voice, all of that came crashing back on him. He admitted he missed her. She'd been a friend. Someone to help him through this strange thing called vacation.

The winds picked up, cooling him as he walked, and he didn't want to turn around. He wanted to make it to the Lighthouse, *needed* to make it there for some strange reason. He felt a hand on his shoulder, a gentle push. He spun around. No one was there. Again.

"Hey. Over here."

He almost imagined he heard Julie's voice calling him. That was crazy. He turned and started to walk back to the inn. No lighthouse this time, he'd better get back before the storm hit.

He felt another twinge on his shoulder, like the faintest resting of a hand.

Turn around and look, Boo.

Now he really was imagining things. But he did turn back towards the lighthouse and swept his glance over the wide beach. A lone woman sat on the sand, waving her arms.

"Hey. Over here. Hey."

That was Julie's voice, he knew it, even as the words broke apart and were tossed in the wind. He paused, uncertain what to do. Susan had warned him to stay away. He should just turn around right now.

Go to her, Boo.

"I hear you, Sunshine. I hear you," he whispered.

He raised a hand in a wave and jogged down the beach towards Julie.

CHAPTER 13

J ulie looked down the beach and saw a lone man jogging towards her from around the bend. He'd heard her, thank goodness. She watched as he got larger as he approached.

Her breath froze in her chest.

Reed?

Seriously?

With all the people on the island, Reed was the one to rescue her?

He jogged over to where she sat on the beach. She saw him look at the blood on the sand and drop down beside her. "You're hurt. What happened?" He looked her over from head to toe.

"I cut my heel on something sharp. I was going to call Tally or Susan, but my phone is dead."

Reed shucked off his shirt, his chest gleaming in

the soft light—not that she noticed. He gently tied his shirt around her foot. "I'll carry you."

"No, I can walk. Just help me up."

He stood and reached down to pull her to her feet. She winced when she put weight on her foot. It was going to be a long walk home.

"You could go get my van and come pick me up." That was an idea. Much better than walking with her foot wrapped up in his shirt.

Reed paled a bit. "I… don't drive."

"Really? Oh. Well, that won't work then, will it?" She stood balancing on one foot. "You could call Tally or Susan."

"Didn't bring my phone. I've kind of gone off the grid this week."

"Well, that's that. Let's walk." She took a tentative step. It hurt a bit, but she could manage. The shirt would at least keep the sand out of the wound. "We should go before the storm hits."

Reed glanced out at sea, looking surprised to see the incoming clouds. "The storm is coming in faster than I thought. We should hurry."

She leaned on him and they headed down the beach. His strong arm wrapped around her, supporting most of her weight. He held her steady and secure. She ignored the fact it felt so very good to be wrapped up in his arm.

Totally ignored it.

"You doing okay? You could sit here and I'd go for

help, but I'm afraid the storm will hit before I can get back."

"No, I'm fine really." She didn't want to sit and have him leave her behind. She wanted to continue to walk down this beach, leaning on him.

The subtle scent of Reed's spicy aftershave drifted around her. Not that she noticed that, either.

Then the rain hit. First a few large drops of rain splattered around them, then it came down and pounded them with its fury.

She stumbled a bit and he caught her as she started to fall. Before she had time to protest, he swooped her up in his arms. "I'm carrying you the rest of the way. I can see the inn from here. We'll get Susan to help you when we get there."

She wanted to protest, to tell him she was fine and she could walk on her own, thank you very much. But... it felt so good to rest against his chest. She could feel his heart beating against her. His bare skin heated her through her thin t-shirt. The t-shirt that was now clinging to her in an almost indecent way.

He bent over, trying to protect her from the worst of the storm. She tucked her head against his neck and clung to him, the rain sliding over them as he hurried towards safety.

Before she could convince herself to tell him to just put her down, he was climbing the steps of the inn. He pushed through the door from the deck and headed into the lobby.

Susan looked up from the reception desk. "What…"

Reed stood with her in his arms, dripping all over the lobby floor. "She's hurt. She's got a nasty gash on her foot."

Susan rushed out from behind the desk. "Is it bad? Are you okay?"

"I'm okay. Reed is exaggerating… I think." There was a lot of blood soaked into Reed's shirt.

"Jamie, can you cover the desk?" Susan called out to her son as he came out of the office to see what the commotion was. "Sure. Everything okay?"

"Yes, I just need to help Julie." Susan turned to Reed. "Can you carry her over to my cottage? It's right outside the kitchen door."

"No problem."

"I can walk."

Susan dismissed the suggestion with a wave of her hand. "No, you can't. Not until I get a look at your foot."

Julie settled back against Reed's chest, savoring the last few moments of him holding her close… even though she'd told him to leave her alone and never come see her again.

Reed was going to have to explain to Susan how this wasn't his fault. Not at all. He'd run into Julie by accident. And it was a good thing he had or she'd still be sitting out there alone, pummeled by the storm. The thought made his heart pound in his chest, and he tightened his hold on her.

He'd fully intended to stay away from Julie. This wasn't his fault. It wasn't. It was just a... nice coincidence. Well, not nice, because Julie was hurt. His thoughts ping-ponged along.

She felt so darn good in his arms. He wished they'd been miles further away and he could have carried her on and on, resting against his chest. Her one arm was wrapped around his neck, and the scent of her hair teased him as drops of rain dripped from her hair onto his bare skin. He wanted to bury his face in her hair, but of course he couldn't do that.

But he wanted to.

He carried Julie into Susan's cottage.

"Set her down on the couch. I'll get the first aid kit." Susan shot him a look that clearly said I told you to stay away.

It wasn't his fault.

He reluctantly walked over to the couch and eased Julie down on it. Her arm slipped away from around his neck. He wanted, more than anything in the world, to just pick her right back up.

Susan tossed him a towel. She sat beside Julie, wrapped another towel careful around her, and opened a first aid kit. "Let me look at this."

"Ouch." Julie winced as Susan cleaned the cut.

"Doesn't look like it needs stitches, but it's going to hurt like all get-out for a few days."

Reed peered over Susan's shoulder.

"Great timing. I'm going to be so busy this week getting ready for Camille's mother's party."

"You really should stay off of that for a few days. I'll use some butterfly bandages to close it and I'll wrap it up, but really, you should give it a few days to heal."

"That's not going to happen."

"You should listen to Susan."

"A lot of people should listen to me." Susan's eyes met his.

Julie looked at Susan, then back at him. "What's going on with you two?"

"Nothing." Reed shook his head.

"Yes, something is. Susan?"

Susan sighed. "I caught him going out to find you. He said he'd figured things out, made his peace, and wanted to... I don't know... date you? But I told him to stay away from you. Really, Julie, he's leaving soon. I don't want you to go through that again."

"I did listen to you. I understood and agreed with you, but I didn't go looking for her. I just found her, hurt, at Lighthouse Point and brought her back here to you. It was a... coincidence." Or fate, he was beginning to believe it was fate.

Julie looked from Reed to Susan. "I think this is for me to decide, isn't it?"

"It is. But... I really don't want to see you hurt again." Susan stood up, then leaned back and settled an afghan around her friend's shoulders. "I'm going back to the inn. You two talk. I'll drive you home and get you settled when you're ready."

Julie sat quietly after Susan left. Reed dropped down beside Julie, alternating waiting for her to say something, and thinking he should speak first.

"You were coming to find me?"

"Earlier I was. Before Susan talked to me. She has a valid point. I am leaving."

"So... you think you've really made peace with your past?"

"I have." He reached for her hand. "I know it's too late, but I have put the past behind me. I'm sorry I didn't figure it out before we... well, I don't know what we are, or what we were going to be. I'll leave the island now. I'll leave you alone, like you asked me to."

"You don't have to leave." Her voice was a whisper.

"But, I should. I honestly don't think I could stay here and not see you."

"I don't want you to stay here and *not* see me." Julie hoped she didn't live to regret her words. "I want you to say here and spend more time with me. I don't know where we're headed, but I know I enjoy being with you."

"I like spending time with you, too." Reed sat on the couch by her side and pulled the fluffy blue towel around her shoulders when she shivered.

But she wasn't shivering from cold. She didn't think a nice dry towel would help her.

"You're sure you've sorted everything out? You won't just... quit again? I mean, I know you leave at the end of the month, but we'll spend time together until then?"

"I'm sure. We'll spend time together. Every day if you'll let me."

"I'd like that."

Before she knew what he was doing, he leaned in and kissed her. The kiss was soft and gentle, and his hand reached up to cradle her face. She reached her hand to cover his and lost herself in his kiss.

He pulled away slightly and smiled at her. "I've been wanting to do that since the first time I met you."

"You... ah... you have?" Her words came in disjointed gasps.

"I have. And you know what?"

"What?" Her world was spinning out of control.

"I'm going to do it again if you don't mind."

"I don't mind." She tilted her head up. "Not one bit."

His lips pressed against hers again and he pulled her close, his heart beating in rhythm with hers.

Reed reluctantly pulled away. "I should go get Susan to drive you home."

Julie looked at him with the most adorably dazed expression. "I... uh... sure."

He smiled at her and tipped her chin up for one more lingering kiss. "I'll be back."

He quickly went to his room and slipped on dry clothes, then met Susan and insisted on riding over to Julie's house with them. There was no way he was going to let Julie fend for herself and hobble around alone in her cottage.

When they arrived, Susan helped Julie change into dry clothes and settled her on the couch. "I'm going to stay with Julie for a while," Reed assured Susan, although she looked more worried at his remark than reassured.

"I could stay." Susan bit her lip.

"No, you go back to the inn. I know you're busy getting everything ready for your big weekend. I'll be fine." Julie leaned back against the pillows on the well-worn couch.

Susan wrinkled her brow. "Okay, but you call me if you need anything. Anything at all. And stay off your foot."

"Thanks for bringing me back home."

Susan nodded and hurried out the door. Reed settled down on a couch next to Julie, then jumped back up. "I should get you something to eat."

"You don't have to do that."

"Yes, I do. And I want to."

"Well, I am hungry. There's a loaf of homemade bread and some sliced chicken in the kitchen if you want to make sandwiches. Oh, and a bowl of fruit salad in the fridge."

Reed went to the kitchen and opened cabinets and drawers. He'd never seen so many pots and pans and different utensils. He didn't even know what some of the pans were used for. The cabinets and drawers looked organized to perfection, no jumbled silverware, no junk drawer. He located the plates and glasses and put together their meal. He loaded a tray he found and carried it back into the front room.

Julie sat with her foot propped up on the coffee table. "I see you found everything."

"I did. Your kitchen is a masterpiece of... well... kitchen stuff."

Julie grinned. "Though I have my old standbys, I'm always trying out new pans or a new pot or two. I really should go through the cabinets and give some away that I don't use much anymore."

"I have one set of pots, and maybe a cake pan—not that I've ever used it. I do have microwaving down to a science, though." He grinned at her and she widened her eyes in mock horror.

"I know, I know. Can you imagine a man can live off of take-out and reheated left-overs from eating out?"

She shook her head. "Sad. Very sad. Even though I'm at the bakery all day, I love to come home and cook a nice meal."

After they finished, he did the dishes and came back to find Julie sound asleep on the couch. He debated if he should wake her and help her back to her room, but he figured she was exhausted and might sleep the night on the couch. He'd just leave her be.

He quietly covered her with a knitted afghan he found on the back of the recliner, leaned down and pressed a light kiss against her forehead, and let himself out the door.

The storm had passed and the evening was clear with stars tossed across the universe, twinkling in the night sky. A sense of tranquility settled over him. He'd worked things out with Julie and all was right with his world.

CHAPTER 14

R eed knocked on Julie's front door before daybreak. He was determined to help her today in any way he could. He knocked again, but there was no answer. He rang the doorbell. Still no answer. He walked around to her back patio and peeked in the window, hoping no one would see him and report him to the police or something.

Maybe she'd already left for the bakery?

He jogged over to the bakery and went around to the back door. There, in the early morning light, Julie was loading up the van, limping as she walked.

"Hey, I thought you were supposed to stay off your foot."

Julie turned at the sound of his voice. "I have work to do. I can't just… sit. Susan picked me up early this morning and dropped me off at the bakery. She knew I wouldn't stay home."

"Let me help you, then. Show me what needs to be loaded up, and I'll do it. I'll ride along and do the deliveries, too."

"Are you sure?"

"I'm sure."

"I'm not going to turn you down. Thank you. I'm walking pretty slowly and I have so much to get finished today. Yesterday's... adventure... put me so far behind."

She led him into the kitchen, and in no time he had the van loaded and they were headed out for the morning delivery run. Susan raised her eyebrows when he walked into the inn's kitchen with the delivery from the bakery, but didn't say anything. She just pressed a to-go cup of coffee into his hands and shooed him back out to the van. They finished the deliveries and returned to the bakery.

"I'm going to make sure we have everything ordered for the party this weekend. Why don't you sit over there and grab yourself whatever you want for breakfast. The very least I can do is feed you."

"The very least." He winked at her, wanting to lean down and kiss her, but not sure how she'd take that with Nancy throwing curious glances their way. "What can I bring you?"

"I'll take an apricot muffin and coffee, thanks."

He went to the bakery counter, grabbed their breakfasts and two steaming mugs of coffee and went back into the kitchen. Julie sat with her head bent over her desk, a pen in hand, scribbling notes. He walked over and leaned close to her ear. "I really would like to kiss you."

She looked up, startled, and he almost dumped the tray with their pastries. He laughed, and Nancy looked over at them again. "Don't worry. I'm not going to."

Was that disappointment he saw flash across her eyes? "Or I could…"

Julie blushed a delightful shade of rosy pink. "Reed, I have work to do. And Nancy is watching us."

He smiled and set her breakfast on the edge of her desk. "What can I help you with?"

"You've done more than enough. I'm going to go ahead and make up a few things for this weekend, everything I can do in advance, so it won't be so crazy on Friday and Saturday to finish up the order."

"I can help with that."

Julie looked doubtful. "I thought you said you can't cook?"

"I can't, but I can follow directions. I can get things for you so you don't have to walk on your foot so much."

Julie cocked her head, looking at him. "That might work. That's actually a good idea. I can use the help."

"I'm a wealth of good ideas, trust me." He grinned at her. "Eat, and we'll get to work."

147

~

Julie was feeling better. Well, her foot wasn't, it ached from standing on it so much all day. Though Reed and Nancy had nagged at her to stay off her foot. Continuously. Reed had actually been a big help today and she felt like she had things more under control. She hoped, anyway.

Tally showed up after the bakery closed for the day. "I've come to whisk you away to Magic Cafe. Susan's going to meet us there. You need to take a break."

Julie looked around the kitchen. She was tired. Reed walked out of the pantry where she'd just sent him to put away a delivery of supplies.

"Reed." A flash of surprise crossed Tally's face, but she quickly hid it. "Good to see you. Didn't know you were here."

"I came to help Julie. Tried to keep her off her feet."

"And how did that work for you?" Tally threw him a wry smile.

"We had a few arguments—she won most of them—but I tried."

"You were a great help." Julie touched his arm and saw a responsive gleam in his eyes. She quickly took her hand away.

"I'm going to take her to Magic Cafe for a girls' outing."

"Sounds like just what she needs." Reed untied the apron Julie had insisted he wear. "I'm heading out now, but I'll be back tomorrow."

"I don't want you to spend your whole vacation working in the bakery. It's your vacation. You're supposed to be enjoying yourself."

"Oh, I am. I assure you." He winked at her.

Julie noticed Tally didn't miss anything in the exchange. She was probably going to be grilled with twenty questions—or a hundred—when they got to Magic Cafe.

Julie walked Reed over to the kitchen door. He leaned in close to her ear and whispered, "I still want that kiss."

And with that, he disappeared out the door, leaving her strangely jangled and confused. She turned around and Tally took one look at her and laughed.

"Look at you. You've totally fallen for that man, haven't you?"

When they got to Magic Cafe, Tally placed a chair across from Julie and insisted she put her foot up. Susan sat down, waving a not-needed menu in front of her face, trying to cool off. The humidity was fierce today and the ceiling fans on the covered the deck did little to chase it away.

The waitress brought over three large glasses of

sweet tea, and Susan pressed the cool glass against her cheek. "I can't seem to get my internal thermostat to settle down these days."

"It happens… more often than not at your age." Tally smiled wryly.

"Thanks for that." Susan took a long drink of the cool tea.

Tally sat quietly and listened to her two friends chat about their day. She was worried about Julie. The girl had experienced more than her share of hurt and desertion in her lifetime. Maybe Reed would be different? He sure seemed taken with Julie. But, he lived all the way across the country. That didn't make for an easy relationship. But she could tell Julie was smitten with Reed.

Tally knew all the words of warning and caution she wanted to give to Julie wouldn't do a thing once the girl had made up her mind about something. She only hoped Julie was being cautious, leaving up some walls around her heart. Though to be honest, that was no way to go into a relationship.

Which was why Tally avoided any and all entanglements with males. There was no way she was going to tear down any of the perfectly crafted walls she'd built to protect herself.

But Julie was young. She needed to experience great love. Know the soaring feeling where your feet didn't touch the ground and every other thought—if not *every* thought—was wrapped up in your happiness with being with this person. Tally had that once. Years ago. But the hurt that went with it? She'd never put herself in a position to have to go through that pain ever again.

"Tally, what do you think?" Susan looked at her.

"I… I'm sorry. I was lost in thought. What were you asking?"

"She was asking if you agree with her, that I should stay away from Reed." Julie shifted her foot on the chair and rolled her eyes.

"I think… that's a choice you have to make for yourself." But what she really wanted to say was run away. Run very far, and very fast. And yet, she also wanted to say grab it with both hands and hold on for the ride.

So she said nothing more.

"I want to get to know him better. We're not really *dating*."

"He just chooses to spend his whole day with you, working in your kitchen." Susan shrugged.

"We're… friends."

"Well, be careful. He's changed his mind before. I don't want to see you hurt." Susan leaned forward. "But, I do want you to be happy, you know that, right?"

"I know. You two always look after me, I appreciate that. But I am being careful. I'm going in with my eyes wide open. I know he says he's dealt with his past, but I'm not convinced, not fully. I will be careful, I promise."

Tally decided it was time to change the subject. "So, how's the foot doing?"

"It aches today. Feels good to put it up for a while."

"Why didn't Reed go get your van and pick you up instead of having you walk back to the inn with it cut like that? I was so surprised when he came in carrying you from the beach."

"He doesn't drive."

"At all?" Susan's forehead wrinkled.

"I guess not. He just said he couldn't drive." Julie looked at the sea for a moment, then back towards her friends. "You know, he doesn't ever drink either. I wonder... well, I wonder if he got a DUI or something, got his licenses taken away. He even turned down Willie's newest concoction. A basil-motonic. It's delicious, by the way."

"Maybe he never learned to drive?" Susan scowled. "If it was a DUI, then... well, I don't know what, then."

"All I know is he said he couldn't go get the van. He couldn't drive."

"That is a bit strange, but people have all sorts of reasons for the things they do. Did you ask him?" Tally moved the chair Julie was using to prop her foot a bit closer to her. Julie nodded in thanks and adjusted her foot.

"No, I didn't ask him. I was too busy hopping on one foot and worrying about the incoming storm."

"You looked like a drowned rat when you showed up." Susan grinned.

"Thanks for that." Julie crooked the corner of her mouth. "Anyway, I don't know what's up with Reed and driving. I assume he'll tell me in time."

"I think you should ask him." Tally thought Julie should get to know all she could about Reed before rushing into some kind of friendship, relationship... or heartbreak.

"Maybe I will." Julie didn't sound convincing.

Julie knew her friends were only trying to help her, and they were worried about her. She couldn't blame them. Reed had ditched her in an on again, off again way. But he swore he'd sorted out his past now.

But does a person ever really sort out their past and make peace with it? Her past came up and tormented her when she least expected it. This, after swearing she'd dealt with it all. Sometimes the past crept up and laughed at her misguided assurances that everything was safely placed behind her.

Sometimes, she was that young girl again, never knowing if she'd still be staying in the same home, same bed, for more than a night or two. Only once did she let her guard down and dream she'd found a family to live with. A real family.

And how had that worked out for her?

Her friends were right. She should keep up a wall of defense. Get to know Reed, but not let him totally in, not let him have her heart. He was leaving, after all. They could just have a little vacation thingie. Or maybe they were just friends. Though she'd never had a friend who kissed like that and made her heart flutter.

She was in over her head already. Might as well admit that.

Susan's voice brought her out of the depths of over-thinking, her specialty, it seemed.

"We've almost got the inn ready for our guests this weekend. It'll be nice to be full for a change. I have some part-time help coming in. I hope everything goes smoothly. I think we even have the elevator working again. Oh my gosh, I hope so. I can't imagine dealing with Camille if the elevator is out. I'm not thinking her mama's friends are the type that like to deal with three flights of stairs." Susan sighed. "How about you, Julie? You all set for catering their party?"

"I think so. Camille called and also ordered pastries for Sunday morning for the people staying at their main house and guest house. Last minute addition, but I expect no less from Camille. I'll just do them with my normal deliveries on Sunday."

"I hope it all goes well for you two this weekend."

Tally pushed away from the table. "I better get my pre-dinner chores finished. Oh, and Julie, don't even think about walking home. Susan drove here and is going to drop you off."

Julie wouldn't think of arguing with Tally. Ever.

~

Reed sat on the balcony to his room and watched the night sky darken. Stars blinked in the far distance. The moon was bright tonight, bright enough to illuminate a few groups of people walking on the beach.

It was so peaceful just... sitting. When had he given up just savoring the moment? How had he let himself get into the constant motion, never-sit-still life? The night air wrapped around him as he stared out at the ocean. A light breeze, the perfect temperature, drifted across the balcony, and the only sounds were the waves and some people talking and laughing on the inn's deck.

He wished Julie was sitting out here with him. He'd like to be sharing this moment of peace and quietude with her. They wouldn't have to talk. He'd like to just hold her hand and be next to her, sharing the moment.

Loneliness swept through him and chilled him to his very bones. He was so very tired of his aloneness. He knew it was time to move on. He felt he was ready, finally, to come out of years of hibernation. With that thought, he felt the loneliness slowly fade away, like a morning fog dissipating as the sun rose.

Today had been such a great day. He'd enjoyed working side by side with Julie. Helping her out. Laughing with her. Teasing her. Watching her green eyes twinkle with amusement.

He played scenes from today over and over in his mind like a movie. He sat up straight, startled at his thoughts… because he was positive he wanted this movie to have a happily-ever-after ending.

CHAPTER 15

By Friday evening, the inn was teaming with guests. Wonderful, paying, much-needed guests. Susan bumped into Jamie, dropped a stack of papers, and clutched her son's arm to keep from falling.

"You okay, Mom?" Jamie steadied her.

"I'm fine. I'd just forgotten how crazy it gets when we have a full inn with almost everyone checking in at the same time."

"We need a better computer system. A faster one. And a couple more terminals so we can check in more people at once." Jamie bent down and scooped up the fallen papers.

"We'll put it on the list of things we need."

Jamie laughed. "Seems all we do is put things on that list, but rarely have the time or funds to actually *do* anything on that list."

"At least the elevator is working." Susan was willing to count every little blessing at this point.

Mandy, their event planner who was working this weekend to help everything run smoothly, came rushing up to them. "We're running low on ice. The ice maker can't keep up. I think every single guest is out at the beach bar and wanting a mixed drink with ice in it. Haven't these people heard of beer or wine? At least those don't take ice." Mandy gave a half smile. "Oh, and the TV reception is out on all of the first floor, I believe."

"Great." Susan sighed.

"I'll go get a load of ice then take a look at the TV system and see if I can fix it." Jamie reached into his pocket and took out the keys to the inn's van. "I'll be back as quick as I can."

"Thanks, Jamie."

Jamie hurried away. Susan felt Mandy's hand on her arm. "Oh, and Susan?"

"I'm afraid to hear what you have to say next."

"I heard some guests talking about meeting at eleven for the breakfast buffet. It was a group of about thirty people. I know you usually close up at eleven, just thought I'd give you the heads up."

Susan tucked a curl behind her ear. "Okay then. We'll plan on keeping the buffet open longer than usual. I'll let the cook know in the morning."

Mandy gave her a quick hug. "It's all going to be okay. These are just little things. And if it helps, I heard quite a few of the guests talking about how charming the inn is."

"That does help. We're hoping to get repeat guests from this weekend if all goes well."

"I bet you will. The outside turned out great, didn't it? It looks magical with the white Christmas lights and the lanterns on the poles around the edge of the deck."

"You had a good idea on that."

"Thanks." Mandy smiled. "Well, I'm back at it. Let me know if I can help with anything."

Susan watched Mandy walk back outside, wondering what they'd do without her. Mandy had been one of Tally's finds. Tally had sent her their way after she found out Mandy had worked as an event planner at a big resort on the East Coast. Mandy had a couple of young kids and only wanted to work part-time, so the alliance had worked out great for everyone. Mandy's knowledge of event and wedding planning had been just what they needed while they tried to tap into more of that business.

"Susan?" Dorothy called from the reception desk.

Susan didn't know what they'd do without Dorothy either, she knew more about the running of the inn than anyone else after years of working here. Susan sighed and headed over to the desk, hoping it wasn't another problem.

It was late Friday night, or more exact, very early Saturday morning. Julie knew she should be sleeping, tomorrow—today— was a big day, but she couldn't turn off her mind. Three times she got up to jot down notes of things to remember to do. The food for the party had to go off without a hitch. It had to be perfect.

She finally got up, made a cup of chamomile tea, and went up to the widow's walk to sit. She hoped the peacefulness of the night air and the tea would help settle her.

She sipped the tea and stared out into the night. It had been such a busy week. She'd gotten everything ready in advance that she could for Camille's party. Reed had shown up each morning at the bakery and helped her all day long. They'd chatted and laughed and gotten to know each other better as the hours went by. They hadn't, however, talked about her foster care days, and he hadn't once mentioned his wife or how she'd died. Or why he didn't drive, for that matter.

Maybe they hadn't gotten to know each other as much as she thought.

Each time Reed had left, Julie had stood by the door, waiting for him to kiss her again, but he hadn't.

Not once.

She wasn't sure what that meant. Had he decided they should just be friends? Had she done something wrong? Well, she'd hired more help and the kitchen had always been filled with people. Nancy had hovered over her, tsk-tsking if she didn't take time to get off her foot. Maybe it was just because so many people were around.

The thing was, she could still feel his lips against hers and how it had made her feel alive. She wanted the man to kiss her again.

After all this ruckus with Camille's party, she was going to sit down and talk to Reed. Really talk to him. Maybe they could take a long evening walk, or have dinner at Three Wishes like they'd talked about before.

Or maybe, just maybe, she'd kiss *him*…

Julie rushed around the bakery kitchen, carefully checking off items on her extremely detailed to-do list. She plotted just when everything need to be done and in what order. So far, things had been going smoothly.

Nancy had dealt with The Sweet Shoppe crowd and Reed had helped her. He took orders, wiped tables, poured coffee, and he'd even learned how to use the cash register.

He actually seemed to be enjoying himself doing all this work. Work for no pay. On his vacation. She shook her head.

They closed The Sweet Shoppe promptly at two

and Nancy and Reed cleaned up the store. Julie kept checking things off her list.

Check. Check. Check.

She was beginning to feel a bit cocky about the whole thing. She had this. Everything was under control. She planned to be a smashing success at the party and scare up a lot more catering business for the bakery.

Julie whirled around at the sound of a tray crashing to the floor.

"I'm sorry." Nancy's face was white. "I have to go. The hospital called. My mom fell. I…" Nancy looked at the spilled mess.

"I've got it." Reed stepped up besides Nancy.

"Go, go." Julie shooed at Nancy. "We've got this. You need to go be with your mother."

"I'm sorry." Nancy took off her apron and Reed reached for it.

"It's okay. Let me know how she is," Julie assured Nancy.

Nancy hurried out the door and Julie looked at her list. The list with Nancy's name written by so many items. Time to regroup. Her heart raced and she pressed her palms against her hips. She could do this. She could.

"I'll clean this up, then you let me know what I can do to help." Reed smiled at her. "It will be fine."

She smiled back at him, but she wasn't sure it would be fine. There was so much to do and she'd planned on Nancy's help and expertise to get it all done. Reed was eager to help... but he was no baker.

Reed did everything Julie told him to do, even when he didn't really know what he was actually doing. He hauled stuff, he measured ingredients, he took things out of the oven. He poured tall glasses of ice water as the heat in the kitchen rose to an oppressive level, even with the air conditioning struggling to keep up.

He paused to wipe the sweat from his face with a dish towel and looked over at Julie. Her face glistened from the heat, and a few wisps of curls escaped her tied-back hair, framing her face.

She looked worried as she stood staring at her list. She bit the end of her pencil and her forehead wrinkled in concentration.

"What next, boss?" Reed walked over to stand next to her. She looked adorable all covered in a fine dusting of flour and flushed cheeks. He wanted to kiss that cheek and wipe away the trail of flour, but he'd promised himself he'd slow down. He didn't want to scare her off... or scare himself off. He had no missteps left with their budding friendship-maybe-relationship.

"I'm going to start baking a lot at once. Can you set an alarm for fifteen minutes for oven one, and twenty-five minutes for oven two?"

He pulled out his cell phone and set the two alarms. "Got it."

She pointed to a tray of... some kind of appetizers. "Put those in that oven."

He did as he was told.

She kept going the rest of the afternoon. Telling him what alarms to set, what trays to pull. He could feel himself slowing down, but there was no way he was going to rest, not when she was like a tireless ball of energy.

"Where are the canapés?" Julie walked up to him.

"The whats?"

"The canapés that should have come out of the oven—" She looked at her watch. "Ten minutes ago."

"Which oven?" He turned around and knew exactly which oven. The one with smoke coming out of it.

She whirled around at the same time, rushed to the oven, and yanked out multiple trays of burnt appetizers.

"Darn it." She dropped the trays onto the counter.

Reed looked at his phone and realized he hadn't clicked start on the last set of alarms. "I'm sorry. I messed up. I didn't start the timer."

Julie sighed. "Can you open the door?"

The smoke detector went off and Julie walked over to it and waved a tray until the alarm quit.

"I've got to come up with something else to make, but the appetizers that are ready need to go over to

Camille's mother's house now." Julie looked at the trays ready to load into the van, each tray precisely covered and a note attached with heating instructions for the servers.

Reed knew he couldn't help with baking more food, but he was not going to let his mistake mess up Julie's big catering order. His heart pounded in his chest and a panic raced through him. He stomped it down. Julie needed him.

"I'll drive the order over."

Julie looked at him in surprise. "I thought you don't drive."

"I don't. Well, I haven't in a while. But I know how to, if that's what you're asking."

"You have a license?" Julie looked at him, her eyes crinkled in doubt.

"I do. I'll get the van loaded up and you give me directions to Camille's place."

Julie nodded, but didn't look convinced.

Heck, he wasn't convinced he could do it, but he was going to try.

CHAPTER 16

R eed tugged the van door open and stared into the driver's seat. A long tear snaked along the vinyl seat. He should fix that for Julie. Get some duct tape.

Climb into the van.

He took a deep breath and swung into the driver's seat, clutching the van keys. He looked down at his hand and talked himself into uncurling his fingers from around the key. His heart pounded as he slowly, ever-so-slowly, put the key into the ignition.

Turn the key.

He looked out the window and noticed Julie's worried expression. He swallowed and turned his gaze back to the ignition. With a burst of determination he turned the key. The van ground to life. He put it in reverse and backed away from the bakery door. Maybe driving was like riding a bike. You never forget how.

Sweat rolled down his face, but he ignored it. He focused on pulling the van out of the alley behind the bakery and out onto the street. At the end of the lane he looked both ways, flipped on the blinker, and turned right. He inched his way out onto the road then drove down the block to the first stop sign. He flicked off the radio Julie must have left on. He needed no distractions.

His breath came in jagged gasps, and it took every ounce of control to concentrate on the road. After checking to make sure he'd plenty of time to enter the intersection, he inched forward and drove through the crossing.

Breathe. Just breathe. You can do this.

He checked the speedometer, glanced in the rear view mirror, the side mirrors, and forced himself to just watch the road. He glanced at the odometer and saw he'd only gone a mile. It seemed like he'd been driving for an hour. His hands gripped the steering wheel in a fight to keep the van moving straight down the road.

He saw the street sign that alerted him he needed to make another turn. He came to a stop and scanned both directions. As he looked to the right he saw a large black truck speeding down street. He froze, suspended in time.

A black truck.

He closed his eyes, unable to move.

A car honked from behind him. Still, he didn't

open his eyes. Another honk blared through the van. He opened his eyes and forced himself to turn the corner, slowly, carefully. Once he turned the corner, he immediately pulled over to the side of the road.

His heart raced and the world swirled around him. Waves of nausea pummeled him. He put the van in park and sat trying to pull himself together. He leaned his forehead against the steering wheel, fighting the fear, fighting the disappointment. He was going to fail Julie. She'd depended on him, and he just wasn't able to do this. Not yet. Maybe not ever.

He opened his eyes at the sound of a rap on the window.

"Are you okay?" Susan stood beside the van with a worried look on her face.

He rolled down the window. "I... well... no."

"I thought you didn't drive."

"It appears that I don't." Reed stared at his hands, his knuckles white from still clutching the steering wheel.

"Then what are you doing with the van?"

"I was trying to deliver Julie's order to Camille's."

"She sent you to do that?"

"I burnt some stuff—all my fault—and she stayed to make more. I was trying to help..."

Susan tugged the driver's door open. "Get out. Get in the passenger seat. I'll drive. You sit. You look like you're about to pass out."

Reed did as he was told, glad to leave that terrifying driver's seat. "Thank you."

"No problem. We'll get this delivered, then I'll drive the van back to the bakery."

"I really appreciate this."

"You need to talk to Julie, though. Don't try driving again until you get some help."

"I thought... I thought enough time had gone by." It hadn't though. The black truck had been his undoing. He shouldn't have tried to drive the first time when so much depended on him.

Susan pulled the van up to the back of Camille's mother's beach house. Reed finally had a bit of color back in his face. That was good. He could help unload the delivery.

Camille came rushing out of the house. "You're late." She stopped when she saw Susan driving the van. "Where's Julie?"

"She'll be over with more in just a bit."

"Are you sure? I told Mama it was risky to take a chance on Julie."

Susan spun around. "Camille, everything is fine. Julie is the best baker on the island, probably in this whole area of Florida. Now Reed and I will bring the food in and Julie will be here soon with more."

Camille's face scrunched in an I'm-still-not-convinced frown. "Well, I do have to go get ready. I sure hope we haven't made a mistake."

Susan gritted her teeth and stayed silent.

"Mama will give her a piece of her mind if everything isn't perfect." Camille turned and marched away, every bit of her southern belle outrage evident in each retreating step.

Reed walked up beside her. "Here, let me get the food inside."

They carried the trays of food in and then climbed back into the van.

"I've messed things up for Julie, haven't I?"

"No, that's just Camille being Camille. I'm sure it will be fine."

"I hope so." Reed turned and looked out the window.

Susan drove the van back to the bakery and Julie came outside.

"Susan?" Julie looked from Susan to Reed, her eyes full of questions.

"Just jumped in to help a bit." Susan got out of the van and handed the keys to Julie.

Reed got out of the van and walked over to Julie. "I'm sorry… I just… couldn't. I tried. I did."

"It's okay, Reed." Julie reached out and placed her hand on his arm.

Reed nodded, then turned around and walked down the alley, his shoulders sloped in defeat.

"What is going on?" Julie watched Reed's retreat.

"I don't think he was ready to drive. I found him pulled over on the side of the road. We delivered your food, by the way. Everything's fine. Now let's get the rest of the food loaded up and you can drop me off at my car. I left it where I stopped to check on Reed."

"I don't understand…"

"I think you'll need to ask Reed."

Julie put the last of the order in the van and took one last look around the kitchen. Everything was back in shape from the disasters of the day. The kitchen was ready for her to come in early and bake the morning order for Camille's mother. She flicked off the light, locked the door, and climbed into the van.

She drove over to the beach house and unloaded the last of the food. Just as she was placing the last tray in the kitchen, Camille's mother came sailing into the room. "Ah, Julie. There's the rest of the order."

"Yes, ma'am. I'll get the trays in the morning when I deliver your breakfast pastries." Julie stood, poised to flee, but wanted to act professionally.

"I'm glad you got here. Camille was worried."

"No need to worry. I said I'd have the order here." Julie looked at her watch. "Did the servers have any questions? I left instructions on each tray for heating the food."

"Well, my lands, I have no idea. I just let them do

their job." Camille's mother looked perplexed. "I guess everything is okay. I've heard my guest complimenting the appetizers, saying everything is delicious."

A huge wave of relief tumbled over Julie. That's what she needed, for people to take notice of her catering.

Camille's mother turned away, then as an afterthought looked back over her shoulder. "Early tomorrow then, right? I have some guests who are early risers."

"I'm be here."

With that, Camille's mother disappeared from the kitchen.

Julie breathed a sigh of relief and headed back to the van. She needed a shower and clean clothes. She needed to get off her foot, too. Then she'd deal with Reed. But this time was different. It wasn't so much he was walking away from her, as walking away from himself. He'd looked so defeated. She was going to track the man down and make him talk to her.

Julie took a long, cool shower, rinsing away the sweat of the day. She really needed to get that air conditioner in the kitchen fixed. It did work better after Reed had fixed the thermostat, but the old unit could barely keep up when the weather got hot. The merciless heat in the kitchen today had just about killed her.

She toweled off and pulled on a simple, light-weight sundress. She didn't have it in her to blow-dry her hair, so she just brushed it, twisted it into a loose braid, and left it to air dry. She slipped on her most comfortable, practical, but so-not-cute sandals and headed over to the inn, determined to find Reed and talk to him. Or, more exactly, get him to talk to her.

She debated driving, because her foot was still sore, but the breeze had picked up and it was a lovely night. She decided to walk since it was such a short distance to the inn.

She pushed into the lobby and saw Susan look up from the reception desk and wave. Julie crossed the worn wooden floor, smooth from years of wear and refinishing.

"Have you seen Reed around?" Julie leaned against the counter.

"Did you walk here? Aren't you supposed to stay off that foot?"

"It's better. Some better. Anyway it's a beautiful night out. But you didn't answer my question."

"I saw him go out to the deck earlier. Not sure if he took a walk, or he's out on the deck. It's a quiet night here. Everyone is over at Camille's mother's party."

"I'll just go out there and look."

Susan reached over and covered Julie's hand. "He

was really shaken when I found him. Maybe if you can get him to talk... well, maybe that will help him."

"I'm going to try."

Julie crossed the lobby and pushed out onto the deck. Muted strings of warm white lights illuminated the area. A couple sat at the outside bar and she spotted Reed sitting at a table by the railing, staring out at the ocean. She squared her shoulders, took a deep breath, and headed over.

"Reed."

He turned around at the sound of her voice.

"Julie."

Julie perched on the chair beside him. "I thought we could talk."

He turned and looked back out at the sea without answering her.

"Please?" She reached over and touched his arm. "Maybe it will help to explain. Why don't you tell me what happened? Why don't you drive?"

He turned and looked directly at her with a look of raw pain in his eyes. A shiver of emotion spun through her at the agony in his eyes. She waited for him to speak.

"I... I killed my wife."

CHAPTER 17

"What?" Julie's eyes widened, and he could see the surprise and maybe hesitation in her eyes. He noticed a fleeting look of panic, like she wanted to run from him. She took her hand off of his arm and the coolness taunted him where the heat of her hand had just been.

He continued on, saying the words he'd never said to anyone. Ever. But every word was the truth. "It's my fault she died. I killed her. I had a business function to go to the night she died. She really didn't want to go, she was exhausted from a long day of work. But I wheedled, and pleaded, and guilted her into going. I said she needed to be there. The truth was, I hated to go to business dinners like those without her. She would waltz into these things, put people at ease, remember everyone's names, and light up the room. That night was no exception." He paused remembering so vividly how Victoria had been just so... *sparkly* that night.

"No one but me knew how tired she was. The dinner ran long and it was late when we got out of there. She drifted off to sleep soon after we got in the car. Suddenly there was this... black pickup truck... coming right at us... in our lane. I swerved to avoid it and he hit the passenger side of our car. My wife didn't survive. If only I'd swerved the other way, maybe everything would be different. Maybe she'd be alive. Or if I hadn't been so selfish and I would have just agreed she should stay home that night. All my decisions and my selfishness caused her death."

Julie's hand was back on his arm, warm, familiar. "Don't you really think the person driving the truck is the responsible person?"

"He is, too. Found out later he was drunk at the time of the accident, but I can't even shower my anger on him... because he didn't survive the wreck either."

"So this is why you don't drive?"

"I tried to drive one more time. To my wife's funeral. I didn't even make it out of the driveway. A co-worker came looking for me and drove me to the funeral. Haven't gotten behind a wheel of a car since."

"That must be so hard. I can see why you don't like to drive now. So you take the bus and taxis everywhere?"

"Seattle is a very advanced city. My company sends cars to get a lot of its top employees. We ride to work in cars with wi-fi and start working on our way to work. The traffic is terrible, so it's a perk some of the companies offer. I live near a market, or my usual driver will stop and let me run in and get some things if I need to. I get food delivered. I just make it work."

"I understand why you'd feel guilty or responsible, I do. But it wasn't your fault. You know that. It was an accident."

Reed let out a long breath. "I know it was an accident, but I still live with the if-onlys.

"I think we all live with our own set of if-onlys." Julie's voice was low and sad, filled with a wistful longing.

He covered her hand with his own and squeezed hers. "I've never told anyone about this. I mean they know she was killed, but not how I blame myself."

"I don't think you should blame yourself. You didn't do anything wrong."

"But I insisted she come with me. I knew she was tired and wanted to stay home."

"You had no way of knowing what was going to happen. We never know in advance what far-reaching effects our decisions might have. That's just life, Reed. Do you think your wife would want you to blame yourself and shut down? Would you want that for her if the situation was reversed?"

No, he wouldn't. He knew Julie was right.

She tilted her head and looked up at him. "So what made you say you'd drive today?"

"Because it was my fault the batch of food got burned. I just couldn't let my mistake ruin your chance with this big order."

"It wasn't your fault. I could have set a timer. I should have been keeping a better eye on things."

"I *told* you that you could depend on me. I let you down."

"Reed, I think you're too hard on yourself." She smiled. "Too hard on yourself about a lot of things."

"Maybe I am. But my decisions that I made, they brought me to where I am in my life." Reed looked right into Julie's caring eyes. "I thought I had made my peace with this. Well, until today. You see, a black truck came barreling down road, and I just... panicked. It all came back."

"It's okay. It really is. I think that's a normal reaction. You should have told me before though. I'd never have let you drive."

"But you couldn't do the delivery and bake at the same time."

"No, I couldn't, but I would have thought of something. I always do." She smiled at him then, a smile filled with understanding and caring.

For the first time in years, he felt a weight roll off his shoulders. Someone else knew his secret, knew what he had to live with day in and day out. And she hadn't turned and run away. He looked down at their hands entwined on his arm, her tanned fingers interlaced with his.

"Do you think you'll ever drive again? Do you want to try?"

"No, I don't plan on it. I think I'm fine being a non-driver."

"And that's why you don't drink? Because of the drunk driver?"

"Pretty much."

"I'm sorry about all of this. It must have been so hard."

"It was." His voice was low and soft. "It still is."

Julie stayed by Reed's side, and they didn't talk anymore, just sat in silence. The night sky darkened and the stars blinked above them. The breeze picked up and she shivered slightly. Reed wrapped an arm around her and tucked her close to his side. His warmth flowed to her and she leaned against him.

It had been quite a day. She really should head back home, but she was so comfortable tucked against Reed. She could feel his heart beating, connecting them in an understanding of all that life could dish out and all it took to survive. She didn't want to break their tenuous connection.

She didn't blame Reed for panicking today when he drove the van. If only he would have told her before this, she could have prevented everything that happened today.

Those if-onlys again.

She lived with her if-onlys, too. The ones she never told anyone, not even Tally or Susan.

She understood exactly how Reed felt. Exactly. Because she felt responsible for someone's death, too, and it haunted her very being.

If-only.

CHAPTER 18

The next morning Julie delivered the promised pastries to Camille's house. Camille stood in the kitchen, much to Julie's surprise. She'd have figured Camille for a late sleeper. Camille was sipping coffee, dressed in a pair of silk lounging pajamas with a silk robe tied loosely at her slender waist. The woman already had makeup on. Did she get up and put it on first thing, then shower, get dressed, and put it on again?

Julie looked down at her t-shirt and shorts. The t-shirt had a red stain from the raspberry sauce she'd stuffed into a set of pastries. She'd barely had time to pull her hair back in a messy knot as she'd hurried out the door early this morning.

Julie reached to set the last tray on the counter and it tipped and dropped on the floor.

Camille screamed.

Julie looked down, silently giving thanks the tray had landed upright. Besides the pastries being a bit jumbled on the tray, they were okay.

"Goodness, Julie. What a klutz."

Julie bent down to pick up the tray and set it back on the counter.

"What are you doing? We can't serve those to Mama's guests. They were on the *floor*."

"Technically they were on the *tray*. The *bottom* of the tray was on the floor."

"Really, Julie. Can't you be the least bit professional? We can't serve those."

"Fine. I'll go get another tray. You have plenty here to get started. It should take me about thirty minutes to be back with replacements." She'd just take some from the counter at the bakery.

"You really should give Mama a discount after all the problems you've had." Camille shook her head. "I warned her."

Delbert stood by Camille's side, sipping coffee but not offering up his opinion. If he had one. Maybe he always just let Camille have her way.

Julie clenched her fists and pasted on a smile. "I'll be back." She grabbed the tray of *ruined* pastries and headed out to the van.

She came back thirty minutes later as promised with new pastries, though she'd been tempted to just bring back the same ones on a new tray. People were milling about the kitchen now as Julie set the new tray of sweets on the counter.

"Julie, we have guests here now. Can you come back tomorrow for all your mess?"

"My *mess?*"

"The trays and things. I don't want you clattering around the kitchen while our guests are here getting coffee and pastries to take out on the deck."

"Fine. I'll come back tomorrow." *Because I have nothing better to do but make another trip back over here.*

Camille dipped her chin with a you-are-excused nod.

Julie turned and walked out the kitchen door, conjuring up all her willpower to keep from slamming it behind her. She wasn't sure that this catering gig had been worth it money-wise or sanity-wise, but then she did hope to get other business from this. Though she could only hope other people who hired her were easier to work with.

Reed stopped by the bakery at two o'clock, hoping to convince Julie to go out with him. Or stay in. Or anything she wanted, because all he wanted was to spend time with her. He pushed open the back door to the kitchen. Julie was sitting at the counter, sipping some tea.

"Reed." Her face lit up in a smile and his heart did an answering skip-hop in his chest.

"Thought I might be able to convince you to go out with me. This afternoon. Tonight. Both." A schoolboy grin spread across his face.

"I'm honestly too tired to do anything. It was some weekend."

"Then how about I cook for you? Well, grill for you."

"You don't have to do that."

"I want to." He reached for her hand. "Let me do this, take care of you."

"I'm pretty used to taking care of myself."

"Humor me. It's only one night."

She lifted her face up and smiled. "Okay. One night. Because I wouldn't want to get spoiled."

He leaned down and pressed a kiss against those lips of hers. She reached up and wrapped an arm around his neck, and he pulled her to her feet and deepened the kiss. He pulled away from the kiss, but kept her wrapped in his arms. He could stand there holding her for the rest of his life.

He stepped back slightly and tilted her face up to his again. Just one more kiss. That's all he needed.

But that kiss lead to two more.

Julie finally laughed and pulled away. "That's not getting us anywhere, is it?"

"Oh, I assure you, it is. You in my arms is exactly where you should be."

He looked closely at her eyes to see if he was moving too fast, scaring her away, but all he saw was a look of... what was that look? It looked dangerously close to a look of... caring. Of a promise of much more than friendship.

Anyway, friends didn't kiss like this, did they?

He reached out and pulled her close to him once again. She tucked her face against his chest and wrapped her arms around him. He whispered as he held her tightly. "You feel so very right in my arms, I want to spend every minute possible with you."

"I'd like that." Her words were like the gentle drops of the first spring rain, bringing him back to life.

Reed did as he promised and made a delicious dinner, if he did say so himself. They went up to the widow's walk after the meal and sat outside, watching the sky burst into brilliant colors as the sun slipped below the horizon. The stars came out and twinkled above them. They sat, simply holding hands and talking.

"How about we go to the beach tomorrow after the bakery closes?" Reed looked over at Julie.

"I could use a break after this busy weekend."

"It's settled then. I'll come by about two?"

"How about I pick you up in the van and we'll go

to the beach at the end of the island. Should be quiet on a weekday afternoon."

"Whatever you want works for me." Whatever she did want, did work for him. He just wanted to spend time with her. Get to know her better. He already knew that look in her eyes when her mind was busy planning things, organizing her to-do list in her head. He knew a t-shirt with a clever saying was her shirt of choice. He knew she liked to walk at the water's edge on beach walks, and that she knew the names of the constellations in the night sky. She liked sweet tea, hot coffee, and Willie's basil-motonics. She had boundless energy in her bakery and endless patience with her customers.

What he didn't know was exactly how she felt about him. She'd at least given him more chances than he deserved, and he was eternally grateful for that. She'd shown patience at his struggle with dealing with his past.

They both avoided talking about the future, the one where he'd have to head back to Seattle and resume his real life. They'd have to talk about it sometime. But not now. Not on this perfect night.

He looked over and saw her stifle a yawn.

"I should go. You're tired after all you did this weekend."

"I am a bit tired. But it's such a lovely night."

"We'll have more nights. Ones where you aren't so exhausted." He stood up and held out his hand. She

WISH UPON A SHELL

placed her hand in his and he pulled her to her feet…
and into his arms. He couldn't help it. He leaned
down and kissed her gently.

She kissed him back and wound her arms around
his waist. He pulled her close and kissed her again.
She tucked her head against his chest and he could
feel her heart beating against him.

This night. This moment. This woman.
Everything seemed so perfect in this moment.

"I think I'm falling for you." The words surprised
him. He hadn't meant to say them out loud. Not yet.

"I… I don't know what to say." Julie looked up at
him, her green eyes wide with surprise.

"Listen, I know you have a right to be leery of me,
to not trust me. I just want you to know that you're…
important to me. You feel so right in my arms. It
seems so right to spend time with you."

"I enjoy spending time with you, too, but I
thought we were going to take things slowly?"

Reed could see the hesitation in her eyes and
regretted his words. The last thing he wanted was to
frighten her way. How had those words escaped,
anyway? He was usually all in control and thought
things through in advance. But this woman made him
loosen his tightly controlled emotions.

"Ah, we did. And we are. I can give you all the
time you need."

Well, he could give her the rest of the month.
Then they would have to make some decisions.

~

Julie walked Reed to the door and kissed him goodnight. A long, thorough goodnight kiss. A kiss that left her nerves jangled after he left. She climbed the stairs back up to the widow's walk and sat alone in the darkness.

So many thoughts whirled through her mind. Tally talking about believing in soul mates. Reed's kisses. Troy walking out on her after she'd finally trusted him. Then there was the whole foster care fiasco. She just didn't think she was ready to trust again, to really believe someone was going to be there for her and stay. She needed more time, only Reed was just here for a few more weeks.

She sighed and stared up at the stars, drawing imaginary lines between them to make up the constellations. She'd really gotten herself into an impossible situation with Reed. She was afraid to truly trust him, but every moment away from him seemed... empty.

She was falling for him, too, not that she'd been able to admit that to Reed. Heck, she could barely admit it to herself.

She hugged her knees to her chest and searched for her answers in the night sky. The sky remained silent.

CHAPTER 19

Reed made sure to fill up every free moment Julie had the next couple of days, and she didn't complain about it one bit. They walked the beach, grilled out dinners, and talked for hours on end. Oh, and kissed. Lots of kisses. Really good kisses. Great ones even.

She sat across the table from him in her tiny kitchen. They'd just raced back from a beach walk, barely outrunning the storm that was now howling around the cottage outside. The doorbell rang, and she got up from the table to answer it.

"Sheriff Dave, how are you? What brings you here? Come in out of the storm." Julie held open the door to her cottage and invited the sheriff inside.

The sheriff stepped inside, dripping rain on the mat by her door. "Sorry about that."

"No, it's okay. Why don't you come into the

kitchen and have some hot tea? It's nasty out there today. Chilly and rainy."

"I, uh." Sheriff Dave shifted from foot to foot. "I need to speak with you. Official business."

"Really? Well, can you talk officially with a nice hot cup of tea?"

"I'd rather not."

The sheriff was acting strange and Julie sensed, rather than saw, that Reed had come up behind her.

Julie looked at Sheriff Dave. His normally friendly face was now carved with seriousness. The sheriff rarely had crucial things to deal with. A few parties gone out of control. Minor complaints of small thefts on the beach. Speeding on Gulf Avenue. A few fender benders. Their island was a pretty safe haven from the realities of the rest of the world.

Julie turned to Reed. "Reed, this is Sheriff Dave."

Reed held out his hand and the sheriff paused before taking it. He withdrew from the handshake and looked at her, his eyes piercingly direct.

"I need to question you."

"Me? About what?"

"I've had a complaint. There was a theft."

"Really, who was robbed?"

"A theft from Mrs. Montgomery's beach home."

"Camille's mother's house? What does that have to do with me?"

"It appears that quite a bit of silver has gone missing from their home. Silver trays, a silver tea service, sterling silverware. Thousands of dollars' worth."

Julie's forehead wrinkled. "I didn't see anything unusual when I was there."

"Camille said the items went missing the morning you came to pick up your trays and things from the event you catered at their home. She said their housekeeper let you in, but didn't stick around to watch you load up."

"And?" Her pulse quickened.

"And Camille thought you might be... uh... a person of interest."

Julie's heart pounded in her chest. *Not again. Not now.*

"So Camille thinks *I* took her silver?"

"We're just talking to all the suspects."

"I'm a *suspect*?"

"We're checking out everyone who was around the house that morning, but their housekeeper has been with them for twenty years and the only other people still staying there were Camille and her mother." Sheriff Dave looked at a small notebook he held in his hand. "No one else."

"Well, someone else was there, because I sure as heck didn't take anything." Julie felt Reed's hand on her arm. It was reassuring to have backup and support, she just wished she'd taken him up on his offer to help her go retrieve the items from Camille's. Then she'd have a witness.

"So, are you accusing Julie of this crime?" Reed moved to her side and wrapped an arm loosely around her waist.

"I'm just checking things out right now. Wanted to know if you saw anyone else there." The sheriff looked at her closely, she could feel him searching her face.

She saw the look in his eyes. The look she remembered. The look that said he didn't believe her. The memories slammed into her and she closed her eyes for a brief moment.

"So, are you arresting me?"

The sheriff stood looking at her. "Right now the evidence is all circumstantial. But I will say it doesn't look good for you."

"Wouldn't you need to find that she actually had the items in her possession to arrest her?" Reed stared down the sheriff. "I believe the law assumes a person is innocent until proven guilty."

"I'm just doing my job. Right now it appears Julie is the only one with... opportunity." The sheriff turned to leave. "I'll be checking things out and will be back with more questions."

Julie swallowed. "I didn't take anything from Camille's house. Not one thing."

"As I said, I'm still investigating."

The sheriff walked out the door and Julie slowly closed it behind him. She sagged against it, as all of a sudden her legs didn't want to hold her weight.

"Are you okay?" Reed moved close and put his hands on her arms, helping to support her.

"I'm... not."

"Here, come sit on the couch. I'll bring in your tea." She sat down as told, her mind racing and the pulse thumping an irregular beat on her temple. She reached up to massage the spot and watched while the room whirled around with every passing second.

This couldn't happen to her again. What if the sheriff checked records? Could he see what she'd been accused of before? It had been so many years ago, a different state. She gulped a big swallow of air.

Reed came back and pressed the warm cup into her hands. She took a sip, willing herself to calm down.

"You didn't take anything, so everything will be okay." Reed ran his hands up and down her arms, warming her. While it did heat her arms, the frigid feeling in her very bones refused to thaw.

"No, it's not always okay when you're accused of something. Sometimes you get the blame, even if you didn't do it."

"But they have no proof."

"That doesn't always matter." Julie knew that guilt or innocence was not always the determining factor on who gets the blame.

The late afternoon storm faded as was usual this time of year, and Reed suggested they go have dinner at Magic Cafe. That sounded okay to Julie. She didn't feel like cooking, didn't really feel like going out, but she probably should eat.

As soon as they got to Magic Cafe, Julie knew she'd made a mistake. A handful of locals eating at the cafe looked up and whispered when they saw her come in. Furtive looks were flashed her way as Tally led them to a table.

"Don't mind them." Tally turned and actually glared at the people at the next table.

"Camille's been talking." Julie said it more in a statement than a question.

"Let's just say a dozen people have asked me if I've heard about the theft, and half of them asked if I'd talked to you." Tally shook her head. "Fools."

"I didn't—"

"Of course you didn't. Camille is a fool to even bring you into this."

"Do you want to leave?" Reed reached out a hand to cover hers.

"You are not leaving here, Julie Farmington. That is not how we deal with gossip. Anyone who believes Camille is a ninny bug right along with her. Dinner is on me tonight."

"You don't have to do that." Julie tried to ignore the people glancing her way.

"I want to. Now, what kind of grouper do you

want tonight? A good grouper meal always makes the world look a bit brighter."

Julie sent a weak smile to her friend. Tally always believed in her and always knew how to cheer her up. "Surprise us. I love grouper every way you serve it."

"Great. And ignore them. They'll move on to new gossip soon." Tally shook her head. "Fools, all of them."

"Come sit next to me on my side of the table. We'll watch the ocean and ignore everyone sitting behind us." Reed patted the chair next to him.

Julie got up and settled in the chair beside him. Reed scooted his chair closer to hers and wrapped an arm around her shoulder. "You've got a great friend in Tally."

"I do. I'm really lucky." Julie looked down at the table. "I feel like everyone is staring at me though."

"At least they only get a view of your back now." Reed winked at her and she tried a weak smile in return. He squeezed her hand. "I think you should ignore them."

"I'm trying."

"I know it's not the same, but after Victoria died I felt like everyone was watching me and whispering about me at work. It's not easy to deal with."

Reed remembered those days vividly, when his every

move, his every expression was scrutinized as if people were waiting for him to fall apart. He'd just continued on with his days, moving in rote motion, day after day. Somewhere in there, people moved on to other things and had forgotten all about how he'd lost his wife, and the looks came less frequently. Then life had just gone on for the rest of the world, but not really for him.

Tally brought their dinner and a nice big glass of wine for Julie. She sipped it as she ate her grouper in silence.

"It is going to be okay. You didn't take anything. They'll find out who did."

"I can't believe Camille would even give my name to Sheriff Dave as a suspect. She's known me since I've moved here. I've been here—I don't know—eighteen, nineteen years? Everyone knows me. I've built my business. I thought that finally, finally I'd found a home. But now…" Julie's eyes were clouded with self-doubt. "I was fooling myself. I'm still an outsider. The first to be blamed. And look at everyone talking about me."

Julie blinked a few times, and Reed was afraid she would give into the tears he knew were hiding just below the surface. He couldn't blame her. "Are you okay? We can leave, really."

"No, finish your meal. I'll be fine."

Just then he noticed the cafe grew strangely quiet. There was no sound of chatter, only the sound of the waves on the shore and a lone bird calling in the distance. He turned around slightly and saw the reason.

Camille stood at the hostess stand. He saw Tally spy Camille and stride towards her.

"What is it?" Julie started to turn around.

"It's… Camille and that Delbert guy."

"I've got this." Julie pushed back from the table, took one more sip of her wine, and stood up. He hastily put down his fork and got up, too. Julie threaded her way over to Camille. All eyes in the restaurant were on her.

"Camille. Delbert." Julie stood right in front of them.

Tally took one step back, crossed her arms, and he noticed a hint of smile on her face, quickly followed by a look of expectation.

"Julie, I didn't expect to find you… out."

"Why? Because of the rumors you've spread around town?"

"I just told the sheriff the truth. You were the only one there when all of Mama's silver went missing. It's been in the family for years. Mama is heartbroken." Camille's voice rose. She acted like she was on stage, and the customers at the restaurant were her audience. She flipped her hair back with one hand and rested the other hand at her throat. "I feel so *terrible* I suggested Mama use you. So terrible."

Reed started to defend Julie, but Tally put her hand on his arm and shook her head slightly.

Julie squared off with Camille, face to face, toe to toe. "You should feel terrible about accusing me of something you know I didn't do. You've known me for almost twenty years, Camille."

"Well, I guess it goes to show we don't always really know people like we think we do."

"I know you, Camille. Too well. You never change. I didn't take your mother's silver."

"There's just no one else who was there, Julie. No one. It had to be you."

"Well, someone was, because I didn't take one darn thing. And when they find who took the stuff, I expect a public apology from you. Which I may or may not accept."

Julie turned to Reed. "Let's go. I've lost my appetite."

"I think it might be better if Camille and her friend here left." Tally took a step forward.

"You are telling me to leave? You're not going to seat Delbert and me?" Camille's eyes widened in disbelief.

"Not tonight, no. I think there's been enough drama for the night. You're welcome back here again after you apologize to Julie."

"I have nothing to apologize for. She's… a *thief.*"

Tally turned to Delbert. "I'd appreciate it if you

took Camille somewhere else for your dinner tonight."

Delbert's face was covered in a tinge of red, and he turned to Camille. "Honey, let's go find someplace else to eat tonight, what do you say?"

"I say fine. I didn't want to eat at this greasy place anyway." Camille spun on her heels and swept out of Magic Cafe.

"Ma'am." Delbert nodded to Tally and hurried after Camille.

"Well, that was interesting." Reed was in awe of the way Julie had handled that, and Tally too, for that matter.

"Interesting, indeed. Now you two go finish your meal. Enjoy it in peace and quiet. Things will settle down here soon."

The customers in the restaurant must have agreed because they all went back to eating their meals and the conversation level resumed.

He placed his hand in the small of Julie's back. "What do you say? Want to finish that meal?"

Julie grinned. "You know what? I do."

"Thought you said you lost your appetite."

"I'm suddenly famished." She grinned at him.

Reed laughed and leaned down a pressed a quick kiss against her forehead. "Come on then. Let's have that dinner Tally so graciously provided."

Julie and Reed sat out on the widow's walk enjoying the night air after their dinner at Magic Cafe. Julie sank into the cozy warmth of a shawl she'd wrapped around her shoulders.

Julie let the events of the day play over and over again in her mind. Was the sheriff going to come back and question her again? What could she say to him to prove her innocence? Someone had to have been there at Mrs. Montgomery's that day.

She looked over at Reed, who was lost in his own thoughts. She wondered if he truly believed she was innocent. She knew what it was like to think the people you trusted believed you... but then find out they didn't.

Reed turned to her and smiled his lazy, sexy smile at her. "You doing okay?"

"I think so."

"This seemed to hit you hard. Harder than I would have expected. I guess because it's a small town and you're worried about your reputation and the bakery?" He reached over and squeezed her hand.

She took a deep breath. "It's not just that..."

"What is it then?" His voice was low and encouraging.

"I... I've been arrested for stealing before."

Reed's eyes widened in the moonlight. "What? When?"

"When I was younger. Seventeen. My foster parents accused me of stealing money. A lot of money." Julie looked down at her short, painted finger nails. She really should touch up the nail polish.

Why was she thinking of nail polish at a time like this?

"Anyway, they called the police. I was arrested. It was the foster placement where the grandmother taught me to bake. I thought I had finally found… a family. I learned though, that no matter what, blood is thicker. I was young and foolish. I knew their son had been stealing money for drugs. But I had the biggest crush on him. I believed I loved him, as only a seventeen-year-old girl can believe. Truly and deeply."

She looked at Reed, trying to read his thoughts. "Mick begged me not to tell them the truth… then he told me it didn't matter because they wouldn't believe me over him anyway." She felt the waves of shame crash over her again. Her foolishness for thinking she was a member of the family, for thinking Mick had loved her, too. The fact she hadn't had the backbone to stand up and defend herself. "So I didn't say anything. Let them accuse me. Took the blame for him."

She looked up at the stars then continued. "I was sent to juvenile detention. They finally let me out and the charges were dropped. I think maybe the grandmother had something to do with that. Maybe. I was sent to another group home until I left the day I turned eighteen."

She could still feel the guilt. "I don't know why I

didn't stand up for myself then. Tell the truth that Mick had taken the money. He'd been swiping money the whole time I lived there."

"You were young and felt betrayed." Reed took her hand in his and brought it up to his lips and kissed it gently.

"I was. But maybe if I had told the truth. Maybe things would have been different. Maybe his parents would have begun to question things. I never told the truth… and Mick ended up dead a year later. He was shot in some kind of drug deal gone bad. If only I had spoken up then, maybe things would be different. Maybe he'd still be alive. It's those if-onlys that get you."

"You can't blame yourself for his death."

A wry laugh escaped Julie. "Ah, that's what I said about Victoria, wasn't it? But you know, we make decisions and they sometimes affect our whole life and the lives of others. We just never know."

"No, we don't know, do we?"

"I've never told anyone about all this."

"I'm glad you told me." Reed wrapped his arm around her and pulled her close. His warmth swept through her in a wave of healing and understanding.

He believed her.

CHAPTER 20

Tally pushed through the door to the outside seating area. The lunch crowd was waning with a few people trickling in from the beach, but most of the tables were empty. She saw Paul and Josephine eating at a table at the edge of the sand. She glanced at her watch and figured she had a few minutes to catch up with her old friend before she needed to run to the bank.

"Paul, Josephine, I didn't see you come in."

"We decided on a late lunch today. Josephine was craving your shrimp salad, and I live to give her what she wants." Paul winked at Josephine.

"Oh, Paul. You do spoil me. Not that I'm complaining, mind you." Josephine smiled at Paul with one of those smiles that shut out the rest of the world and was meant for one person only.

Tally could barely remember when she'd been on

the receiving end of that kind of smile. It had been a lifetime ago, it seemed. But she was glad to see Paul and Josephine had that kind of relationship, especially since it had been years and years in the making.

"I heard that Camille Montgomery has been stirring up trouble here. Her mama lives in Comfort Crossing, Mississippi, where my family is from, did you know that?" Josephine turned her attention from Paul to Tally.

"Paul mentioned it."

"She certainly has a way of causing problems. My niece, Bella, was telling me how Camille caused all sorts of trouble for Hunt's girlfriend, Keely. Hunt, he's the photographer who is going to have a showing at Paul's gallery soon."

"I'm not surprised. Camille seems to be at the center of a lot of drama. I'm annoyed she'd even dream of accusing Julie of taking the silver, though. That is complete and utter nonsense."

"Paul says he's known Julie since she came to the island and that there is no way she had anything to do with the silver's disappearance." Josephine shook her head.

"I'm sure she didn't." Paul's eyes crinkled in concern. "I've heard the business at her bakery has dropped off since Camille started all this gossip."

"It has, and I'm worried about it. Julie's so stressed, I wish I could do something to make things better for her." Tally sat down across from the couple.

"I heard you ran Camille and her man friend out of Magic Cafe the other night." Paul grinned.

"I didn't exactly run them off. I just said she was welcome after she apologizes to Julie." Tally shrugged. "I doubt that will ever happen, knowing Camille. She was making such a scene at the cafe, too. Like she was center stage at her own drama. I figured it was better if she ate somewhere else."

"You know, I think I'll talk to Julie about doing the catering for my gallery events this summer, now that she's getting her catering business going." Paul looked thoughtful.

"I'm sure she'd really appreciate that. She's had quite a few cancellations for catering since all this nonsense Camille is spreading around town."

"Like anyone should believe Camille over Julie." Paul shrugged matter-of-factly.

"Camille has a way of sounding convincing, or at least raising her voice if she thinks you aren't agreeing with her. Sheriff Dave could put a little more effort into trying to find the actual thief, too." Tally sighed. "I better run. Need to get to the bank. It was good seeing you two."

"Good seeing you, Tally. We'll have to all get together soon, if I can convince you to take a night off." Paul smiled. "Not that it happens often."

"You could probably persuade me. I haven't taken a night off in a long time."

"Okay then. We'll set something up. Maybe next week?"

"Next week sounds good." Tally wondered if the evening would actually happen. Half the time when they planned to get together, something would come up at the gallery or at Magic Cafe and they'd have to cancel. "Let's really try and make it work."

Tally walked away from the table, her mind already on the list of errands she needed to run before heading back to Magic Cafe for the dinner crowd.

Reed spent two days watching Julie's business tank and saw the fear in her eyes. She tried to hide it from him, from everyone, but he knew it was there, always riding just beneath the surface. He told jokes to make her smile. He spent each evening with her at her cottage—she said no to going out again, the talk and the stares were just too much.

But mostly he saw the panic in her eyes about her slowly declining business. There were only a few tables filled today at lunch, though her first-of-the-morning customer, Dan, had come in not only for breakfast but for lunch each day in a one-man stand in solidarity.

Reed decided he was done waiting for Sheriff Dave to figure out what a mistake he'd made.

He trotted down the beach, heading towards Camille's mother's beach house. Someone else had to have been there that day when the silver went missing. It was obvious Sheriff Dave thought his job was finished, and he just needed to catch Julie with the silver. Which, of course, would never happen. In the meantime, her business was suffering through no fault of her own. He couldn't bear to see her like this, so beaten down and looking like she was waiting for the other shoe to fall. He couldn't blame her after what had happened to her as a kid in the foster system. No one believed her innocence then. Most of the town had judged her guilty this time.

It ended now.

He strode back and forth on the beachfront by Camille's house and a few of her neighbors. A strong wind buffeting him as he paced. Another storm was coming in. He'd made a lame excuse to Julie about working on his smartphone app tonight. He didn't want to get her hopes up, but he couldn't just stand by and do nothing.

He looked at the beach houses standing regally in a row, each one a little bigger and fancier than the next. It didn't look like anyone was home at any of the houses. A gardening crew was trimming some privacy bushes in front of Camille's neighbors, but no signs of occupants. No one in their swimming pools, no one sitting on chairs on the beach.

He sighed. Enormous houses, just sitting empty

most of the time. He stopped and stared at them, then laughed out loud.

That was it.

He headed off to find the sheriff.

Julie walked into The Lucky Duck. She wanted a cold drink, and with any luck—it was The Lucky Duck after all—she could sit at the far end of the bar and no one would notice her. She was tired of the stares and whispers this week. Business had dropped off at the bakery the last few days and she'd like to blame it on the slow season, but she knew better. People were avoiding her. Well, most people, except Dan Smith. His daily support at breakfast and lunch had meant so much to her. When he'd left today he'd told her to "buck up, kiddo. It will all blow over." She hoped he was right.

She slipped onto a barstool, the very farthest one down the bar. Willie came over and plopped a drink in front of her. "A basil-motonic, on the house."

Julie sighed. "I guess you've heard."

"Sweets, I'm pretty sure everyone in town has heard. Camille doesn't leave much to chance. She's like a one-woman gossip announcer. Don't pay her any mind, though. It will all die down soon.

"Die down… like my business the last few days. I even had two cancelled catering orders."

"You're kidding. Who would ever listen to and actually believe Camille?" Willy shook his head.

"Sheriff Dave, for one."

"Nah, even old Dave can't believe her. He's just doing his job."

"Maybe. He seemed pretty serious when he came to question me as—what did he call me—oh, yes, a person of interest."

Julie sipped on her drink as Willie waited on more customers. In here, no one really paid any attention to her, which suited her just fine. Maybe she'd make this her new hangout.

She sensed someone slip onto the stool next to her and turned to see Jamie sitting there. "Hey, Jamie."

"Jules, drinking your problems away?"

"I wish it was that easy."

"I'm pretty sure even Willie's soon-to-be-famous basil-motonic won't make Camille disappear." Jamie waved to Willie, pointed to Julie's drink and gave a quick me-too flick of his hand.

"Mom talked to Tally. I hear she sent Camille away from Magic Cafe. Probably just fueled the fire with Camille."

"Probably, but it made me feel better." Julie flashed a small smile.

"Well, if it makes you feel any better, Mom is still arguing with Camille about the bill for the extras she ordered for the guests she sent to stay at the inn. Thinks we should just comp all the gift baskets and be grateful she sent guests our way. Honestly though, expensive wine, fancy chocolates, cheese, crackers, bottled sparkling water? We can't afford that for all of our guests. We usually have one bottle of sparkling water and a package of chocolates. That's it."

"And yet, that doesn't make me feel better. I'm not surprised, though. Camille has always acted so entitled. I'm sorry I ever agreed to cater their silly party."

"Mom is beginning to regret she gave Camille a deal on room prices for last weekend, too. Between that, then not wanting to pay for the gift baskets, we'll have barely broken even on the weekend with the extra help we hired."

Willie walked up and set a drink in front of Jamie. "You two eating or just sitting with a drink?"

"I'll have a burger and fries." Julie realized she was famished, she wasn't sure she'd eaten all day.

"Same here." Jamie reached for his basil-motonic and took a sip. "Man, that is just a great drink, Willie."

Willie grinned. "I think it is, too. I'm pretty good at this drink creation thing, aren't I?"

Julie laughed. "And modest. That's what we like about you."

Two young blonde women walked in The Lucky Duck. Willie winked at Julie. "I best go show those two some hospitality."

"You best." Julie flashed him a grin. Willie would

212

never change. Good guy, but with a definite eye for the ladies.

"So where is your man friend tonight?" Jamie reached for a handful of pretzels and nuts from the bowl on the bar.

"My man friend? Is that we're calling him?"

"What do you call him?"

Good question. Boyfriend? Just a friend? *Buddy*?

"How about we call him just Reed? And he said he was busy this evening."

"Just-Reed will work." Jamie said it like it was all one word. "You know, I am sorry about the whole Camille mess. Anyone who knows you, knows that you didn't take the silver."

"And yet, I seem to be the only suspect."

"They'll figure it out."

"It doesn't seem like Sheriff Dave is much interested in finding out who really did it. He has his prime suspect. I imagine he's just hoping to turn up some proof."

"Well, that won't ever happen, so he's going to have to admit he failed to close the case, or get off his duff and find the real thief."

"I can only hope it's sooner than later, or my business is in real danger."

"I'm sorry, Jules. Things will pick up as soon as tourist season starts."

"But I'm afraid with a rumor like this hanging

over me and my catering business, I'm not going to have much of a stellar season."

"I'm sorry. I wish there was something I could do to help."

"There isn't anything. I just have to hope they find the real thief soon, before my business is ruined."

CHAPTER 21

"I've got a great idea for this afternoon." Reed helped Julie clean up after the last customer left the bakery after the breakfast rush. Though there had been nothing *rush* about it. She'd only had a handful of tables filled. He wanted to erase that haunted, worried look from her face.

"What's that?" The corners of Julie's mouth turned up with a meager attempt at a smile. Exhaustion hung on each of her words.

"Susan and I were talking. She said we could take their boat out this afternoon if we wanted. Bet you didn't know I grew up on a lake. Boats are in my blood." Boats were one thing he knew. Too bad he couldn't take boats everywhere. They weren't scary to drive. Boats don't come out of nowhere and kill you. There was plenty of ocean for everyone.

"Oh, I don't know. I should stay for the lunch shift."

"I bet Nancy can handle it."

Julie tossed him a wry smile. "The sad thing is, she probably can. We'll be lucky to get another handful of customers."

"So you'll go?"

"I don't know. I have so much to do. I need to see what I can figure out to get some more catering business. I think I'll run some ads on the Sarasota website and maybe with some of the rental agencies on the island."

"I think you need a break."

"I really shouldn't." Julie looked torn.

"Come on. You know you want to. You don't want me to go alone do you?" Reed put on his best please-please-please face.

Julie laughed. "Okay, I give up. I'll go with you."

"Great, I'm going to run by the inn. Susan said she'd pack us lunches."

"Let me finish up here and I'll pick you up at the inn in about thirty minutes. I'll drive us to the marina."

"Perfect." Reed walked out of the bakery whistling, proud of himself for convincing Julie to take the afternoon off and go for a boat ride with him. The ocean was calm today, and Susan had told him about an island not too far from shore. The small island wasn't developed, but people went there for its beautiful beaches and great shelling. He was going to give Julie a special day she wouldn't soon forget. And, with any luck, she'd leave her troubles behind her for a few hours.

~

Julie didn't really feel like going for a boat ride, but she hadn't wanted to disappoint Reed, and it probably would do her good to get away for an afternoon. It was so scary to think that Camille's rumors had hurt her business so much, and Julie had no control over it. She remembered feeling that same sensation of her world spinning out of control when she'd been arrested as a young girl. But she was an adult now. She'd stood up for herself and proclaimed her innocence, not that it had done her any good.

She decided she was going to put all thought of her problems out of her mind and just try to enjoy the afternoon. She swung by her cottage and put on her swimsuit, then slipped on shorts and a t-shirt over the suit. She grabbed her sunglasses and drove over to the inn.

Reed and Susan were sitting on the front porch chatting as she pulled up. Reed waved, pushed off his chair, and picked up a large picnic basket. Susan stood and they walked down the steps to the van.

"I gave Reed the boat key. He assures me he's an expert, but I know you know how to run the boat, too. I think it's great you're going to get away for a while." Susan handed her a beach blanket.

Reed put the picnic basket in the back then climbed into the van. "You ready for this?"

Julie forced a big smile. "You bet." She saw Susan looking at her and knew she'd been busted. "It'll be fun." Julie sent Susan a don't-say-anything look.

"Yes, you two have a good time. Reed, take care of her. Make sure she has a great afternoon. She deserves it."

"I will. She'll have a great time. I promise."

"Okay, okay you guys. I'll have a good time." Julie held up her hands in surrender. "At least I promise to try."

"Looks like a beautiful day for it. The ocean is calm. I told Reed about Blue Heron Island."

"I haven't been there in forever."

"That's because you never take any time off." Susan cocked an eyebrow.

"Looks who's talking. You want to come with us?"

"Me?" Susan laughed. "No, I think I'll let you two go alone."

"Thanks for the loan of the boat."

"No problem. We don't get out on it very often anymore." Susan gave a pat to the side of the van. "Off with you two. Have fun."

Julie pulled away from the inn and took a shortcut across the island to the marina. They grabbed some cold sodas, water, and ice from the shop at the marina and carried their things to the boat.

Reed climbed onto the boat and held down a hand to help her onto it. He looked around the boat and grinned. "So nice to be on a boat again. She is fabulous. You can tell someone spent a lot of time refurbishing her."

"That was Jamie's uncle. He loved this thing. It was in such bad shape when he bought it. Rebuilt the engine, restored the seats, re-painted it. Named her The Lucky Lady."

Reed laughed. "Of course he did. Wouldn't want to let an opportunity to use the words wish, luck, or lighthouse pass by."

Julie grinned. "Susan and Jamie don't take her out often these days, but we all had some good day trips over the years. Jamie taught me to drive the boat and all about boat safety."

"She's a beaut."

Julie pointed at one of the padded seats. "There's a cooler under that seat."

Reed put the bottled water and sodas in the cooler and dumped the ice on top. "I think we're all set."

Julie untied the boat, and Reed skillfully maneuvered the boat out of the slip and headed out of the marina. A short ride up the inland waterway led them out into the bay between Belle Island and the mainland. Reed increased their speed as they got further into the bay, and the breezes blew her hair this way and that in a joyous dance of freedom. It had been so long since she'd been out on the boat. She could feel her troubles blow away in the breeze. For this one afternoon, she was going to put all her problems behind her.

She turned and smiled at Reed. "This is great, isn't it?"

"It is. I haven't taken a boat out in years. Not sure why. Just never made time for it." He laughed. "Well, that and I'd have to have someone drive me to the marina."

A laugh bubbled up in her. It was good to see Reed relaxing, talking about his inability to drive a car, and joking about it. Maybe someday soon he'd be able to drive again without panicking. She hoped so.

"So you know the way to this Blue Heron Island?"

"I do. Head out of the bay, then turn southwest. It's a few miles out, about five, I think. It's so beautiful there. Long stretch of white sandy beach. Lots of shelling."

They passed from the almost lake-like smooth water of the bay and out into the ocean. The gulf was calm now, though, with just some small swells. She wasn't much of a high surf boater, so today was perfect.

She stood beside him at the helm, feeling the rise and fall of the boat, the wind against her cheeks, and the salty-tackiness of her skin.

They road on in silence. She watched the birds

swoop overhead and the sunlight bounce off the waves and break into a million sparkling diamonds. They reached Blue Heron Island and she pointed to the far end where there was a small cove with shallow water. "There's a small pier in the cove. We can tie up there."

Reed steered to the pier and they secured the boat. Julie filled a small cooler with some of the water, soda, and ice. Reed grabbed the picnic basket and they headed to the shore. Julie was glad to see no one else was around on the island. They walked down around the bend and spread out their beach blanket under some trees on the ocean side of the island.

"You up for a swim?" Julie looked at Reed.

"Sure am." Reed tugged at the back neck of his t-shirt and shrugged it off.

She tried not to stare at his tanned chest. "I, uh, good. Let's swim."

Reed tried not to stare as Julie shrugged off her t-shirt. The shirt was emblazoned with big pink letters that said, "Did your wish come true?"

Pretty much it had.

Julie slipped off her shorts, revealing a modest two-piece purple swimsuit. She dropped her shorts on the blanket and laughed. "Last one in is a rotten egg." She took off running towards the water's edge, her tanned legs spraying sand behind her as she raced to the surf.

He shook his head, grinned, raced after her, and plunged into the surf.

Julie popped out of the waves and pushed her hair back with both hands, laughing. "I win."

"You did. You win the prize." He grinned slyly at her.

She looked at him, her eyes filled with merriment. "What prize?"

"This one." He swung his arms wide and scooped up an armful of water and splashed her.

"Hey." She stumbled backwards then dove underwater.

He spun around to see where she would come back above water, when he felt her jump onto his back. He fell sideways and they both went splashing into the water.

They splashed around in the surf, laughing. Each laugh was like someone was putting a bit of life back into him. The sun glistened off Julie's wet hair. She grinned and frolicked like a kid on her first trip to the ocean.

They finally exhausted themselves with horseplay and waded to the shore and up the beach to their blanket. She handed him a towel, and he dried off a bit before he dropped onto the blanket. She knelt beside him and started unpacking the picnic basket.

"Susan must have thought we were staying for a week. Look at all of this food."

Reed was ravenous, he figured he could make a good dent in the provisions. He reached for a sandwich and bumped hands with Julie. She looked up, smiled, and handed him a soda. He reached for it and noticed she paused, just slightly, before she released the can into his hands. He popped the can open and took a long, cold swallow. And another.

Julie took a half a sandwich and a bottle of water and sat cross-legged on the blanket. "This is so good. I love the inn's sandwiches."

"On your bread, I'd bet."

"Well, there is that." Julie laughed.

The ocean water had dried to a slightly sticky feeling on his skin, but the breeze kept him comfortable. Julie entertained him with stories of people in the town and explained how crazy busy it was during the tourist season in the summer, then again in January through March with people coming to the island to escape the winter.

He didn't know how long they sat talking, or when he'd rested against the tree trunk and Julie had leaned against his shoulder. He loosely wrapped his arm around her shoulder and realized he was trailing his finger up and down her tanned arm resting against him.

She stopped talking then and turned her face up to him. He looked at her, memorizing the moment, her sun-kissed cheeks, her parted lips, her green eyes that looked so trusting. He leaned down and kissed those lips. Gently. Questioningly.

She kissed him back with a softly whispered, "Oh."

She turned slightly and wrapped her arms around him. He pulled her closer and deepened the kiss. His heart pounded in his chest and his breath quickened. This woman touched his heart in a way he thought would never happen again. His cold, frozen, protected heart began to melt.

He finally pulled away. "I… that was nice."

"It was." Her voice was low and wispy. "Reed… um… I think I'm falling for you, too."

"Well, that's fine by me. Perfect even." He kissed her again, content with his life, content with this woman in his arms. The woman who had just said she was falling for him. Which was a good thing, because he was totally taken with her.

He leaned back against the tree and pulled her close to his side. She nestled against him and reached over to entwine her fingers in his. He sensed, more than knew, that they were drifting off to sleep, and it felt so right with her here in his arms.

CHAPTER 22

"**R**eed."

He opened his eyes, trying to focus and figure out where the heck he was.

"Wake up."

He blinked again and saw Julie kneeling before him. His arm was asleep and he shook it and rubbed it.

"Hey." He flashed a lazy grin at her.

"We need to go. Look, a storm is coming in."

He looked out at the ocean and saw the dark clouds gathering in the distance. White caps tripped across the waves now. He scrubbed his hands over his face, coming fully awake. "You're right. We should hurry." He jumped to his feet and started gathering up their things.

Julie dumped the remains of their lunch into the

picnic basket. He grabbed the blanket and cooler and they hurried to the cove.

When they got to the cove, Julie looked up at the sky. "Maybe we should wait it out here. I'm not much of a boat person on rough seas."

"There's not much shelter here. I think we can make it."

"Are you sure?" She looked doubtful and glanced back to the grove of trees behind them.

"I'm sure, come on." He reached out a hand to steady her. "Jump on."

He untied the ropes and climbed on after her. He started the engine and pulled away from the pier. The waves were rough as they pulled out of the cove. "Why don't you sit down here next to me?"

Julie didn't argue. She sat in the seat and grasped the side of the boat. He noticed her knuckles were white where she clasped the seat beneath her.

About halfway back to Belle Island, the heavens opened up and started pounding them with rain. The surf grew wilder and the boat tossed back and forth on the waves. He concentrated all his energy on steering them safely to shore.

"I think I'm going to be sick."

He looked over at Julie. She started to stand up.

"No! Don't stand up."

She staggered to her feet and grabbed hold of his arm. He tried to steady her and steer the boat at the same time. He lost his concentration on steering for a split second to steady her and they hit a wave cockeyed. Julie slipped out of his arm as the boat dropped away, seeming to fall through space. He could see her fall and he swore it was in slow motion. He reached for her again, but he couldn't catch her.

"Julie." He yelled her name over the storm.

Julie lay motionless on the floor of the boat. He didn't dare let go of the wheel to bend down to check on her. He concentrated on maneuvering the boat through the storm, steering their way through the rising waves, racing to Belle Island.

He thought he heard a small moan from Julie. "Julie?"

"Ah… ouch."

"Don't move. Stay down. We're almost to the bay."

Julie curled up into a ball at his feet. His heart pounded and he gripped the wheel. He wanted to reach down and comfort her, to scoop her up in his arms, but he focused on the important job at hand, getting them to safety. He steered the boat into the bay. It was calmer than the ocean, but not by much. He spotted the inlet to the marina and headed there. After what seemed like hours but was probably more like minutes, he pulled the boat into the slip and tied her up.

He finally leaned down over Julie. "Are you okay?"

"I. My head." Julie reached up and touched the back of her head.

"Come on. I'm going to take you for help."

"I'm okay."

"We'll have someone with a bit more medical knowledge tell us that." He leaned down and scooped her into his arms. He climbed out of the boat and rushed down the pier to the parking lot. "The keys. Where are the keys?"

"My pocket, but—"

"I've got this. Give me the keys."

He pressed the keys into the palm of his hand. He unlocked the van and put her in the passenger seat. His heart pounded and guilt washed over him. They never should have tried to outrun the storm. What was he thinking? He should have listened to Julie and found shelter on the island until the storm passed. He knew nothing about gulf coast storms.

He slid into the driver's seat, clenched his teeth, and turned on the engine. He pulled out of their spot and headed down the road towards the emergency clinic he'd seen on Seaside Boulevard.

His pulse pounded and his knuckles were white where he grabbed the steering wheel. He ignored all of that. He focused on keeping the van on the road. The wipers were struggling to keep up with the downpour of rain. He leaned forward, concentrating.

You can do this. You can do this.

He repeated the words like a litany of wishes to the lighthouse.

He swerved to avoid a flooded part of the road and Julie let out a whimper of a moan.

"Hang in there. We're almost there."

He pulled up to the front door of the emergency clinic and flung open his door. He rushed around to Julie and swept her into his arms. He pushed through the doors to the clinic. "I need help here."

A man and a woman in scrubs rushed forward and showed him to a room where he carefully placed her on an examining table. "She fell. Hit her head. On the boat."

"We've got her. Why don't you go move your van?" A kind nurse touched his arm. "She'll be okay. Really. We're going to check her out. Park your van and I'll come out to the waiting room with some paperwork for you to fill out."

Julie's eyes were closed and he didn't like the pale color to her skin.

"She's Julie Farmington."

"I know her. We'll take good care of her." The nurse led him to the doorway.

He walked down the hallway, dripping water with each step. He exited the front door and stood in the pouring rain. He looked up at the sky, taunting him. He'd insisted she come with him today when she hadn't really wanted to go. And she'd asked him to wait out the storm on the island, but he'd insisted they could make it back to Belle Island. This was all his fault. Once again he'd gotten his way, wheedled until Julie agreed. Now, look where it had gotten them. Julie was hurt.

All. His. Fault.

He clenched his jaw, climbed into the van, and slowly pulled it into a parking space. He walked back inside. Another worker offered him a towel and some scrubs to change into so he could get out of his wet clothes. He stood in another exam room and tugged at his wet clothes that were glued to his skin. He sucked in a deep breath and wrestled off his swimsuit and t-shirt, resisting the urge to hurl them across the room when he finally freed himself. He slipped on the dry scrubs and towel-dried his hair.

He glanced at his reflection in the mirror and saw the haunted look in his eyes, the fear etched on his face. Julie just had to be all right, she had to.

Julie slipped in and out of knowing what was going on around her. She would swear at one point she was in the back of the van and the van was going... somewhere. How did Reed manage all this driving? Then her thoughts drifted away and disappeared into the night.

A pounding headache woke her, and she gingerly

opened her eyes. She'd no idea where she was. She struggled to sit up a bit in the bed she was in.

"Sh. Stay still." Reed's voice drifted towards her.

She closed her eyes again, hoping it would make the room quit spinning. She reached up and touched her head and felt a bandage of some sort.

"You hit your head. A concussion and a few stitches."

She tried to remember what happened. They'd been out on Blue Heron Island, having a wonderful time. She'd finally told Reed that she cared about him. She remembered that part. Then that storm had come in. They'd left the island, but the rest of it was hazy.

"Reed?"

"I'm right here."

She felt him take her hand.

"What..."

"We were trying to get to Belle Island before the storm hit. I should have listened to you. We should have just stayed on the island and waited out the storm. It got really rough. You fell and hit your head."

"Where... am I?"

"You're in the hospital on the mainland. I took you to the emergency clinic on Belle Island and they called an ambulance to bring you here. You gave me quite a scare."

"I... don't remember much."

"That's okay. Just take it easy. The doctor said you might not remember everything. It's okay."

"Julie!"

She heard Tally's voice and tried to open her eyes a bit, but that just made her head throb. She sensed Tally at her side and felt Tally's hand brush her hair back. "I came as soon as I heard. Thanks for calling me, Reed."

"No problem. I knew you and Susan would want to know."

"Susan will be here soon."

Julie felt Tally take her hand and Reed, on the other side of the bed, let go of the hand he'd been holding. She wanted to tell him no, hold on to her, but the words tangled in her mind.

"Is she going to be okay?" Tally's voice was tinged with concern.

"The doctor said it was a bad concussion and she needs to take it easy for a few days. She has a few stitches. I'm so sorry…"

"What are you sorry about?"

"It's my fault. Julie didn't really want to go to Blue Heron Island. I talked her into it. Then, I insisted we could outrun the storm coming in. She wanted to stay on the island and wait out the storm. Then she got hurt… and it could have been so much worse. I was so wrong."

Julie wanted to say something, to tell him she *had* wanted to go with him and the break had been so nice. Wanted to tell him again that she cared about him… that she *loved* him.

Oh my gosh, she loved him.

She needed to tell him right now, but the words wouldn't come, they stayed wrapped up in her mind and she drifted off to sleep, knowing Tally and Reed were right there with her.

CHAPTER 23

Susan drove Julie home the next day. Julie wondered where Reed was, but then she was sure he didn't want to drive all the way to the mainland. Tally had told her how Reed had driven her from the marina to the emergency clinic.

Julie leaned on Susan as they walked up the pathway to her house. Susan got her settled on the couch, fussing over her.

"I'm fine." Julie rested against the pillows Susan had placed at the end of the couch for her. "I'll be fine. I know you have the inn to run. Speaking of which, I should check in on the bakery."

"You'll do no such thing. You know what the doctor said. Take it easy for a few days." Susan pinned her with a listen-to-me glare. "Tally went by and checked on things for you. Nancy and your new worker have everything under control. Give it a few days before you go back."

"I can't just sit here."

"Yes, you can, and you will. I mean it. I'll stay here twenty-four seven if I have to."

"No, you have work to do. I'll be good, I promise." Julie looked up and grinned at her friend. "But I might not listen to you the next time you tell me I need to take an afternoon off. This one didn't turn out so well."

"Did you have a good time before the storm?"

"I had a wonderful time." Julie looked at her friend. "I... like Reed. A lot. I had the best time with him. We had... fun. We talked and laughed. I felt so at ease with him and so connected. Susan, I think... I know... that I love him."

"Ha, then it was a good idea to go. Well, not the whole concussion part. You might try it without that next time." Susan smiled at her. "I knew you were falling for him. Knew it. He seems like a good guy. It's nice to see you interested in someone again."

"Where is Reed? I kind of thought he'd be here when I got home."

"I'm not sure. I'll see if he's at the inn when I go back there and tell him I've got you all settled in."

That would be nice. She wanted to see him again. To be honest, she wouldn't mind if he decided to kiss her again. Wouldn't mind that a bit.

"I'm going to fix you a sandwich and some tea before I go."

Julie figured there was no use arguing with her friend. Susan came back with a tray with the food and placed it on the coffee table right by Julie.

"Do you have your new cell phone to call me if you need anything?"

"Yes, it's right here."

"Okay, call me. For anything. Or just to talk."

Julie smiled. "Go. Go run the inn. I'll be fine."

"Okay, but I'm going to check in later this afternoon."

"Of course you are." Julie started to shake her head, but decided that just made her head ache a bit. "If you see Reed, you'll tell him I'm home?"

"Sure will."

Susan let herself out the door and Julie settled back against the pillows. Maybe she'd just take a little nap before eating her sandwich.

Reed stood looking out the window in his room at the inn. The guilt over Julie's accident swept over him... and it felt so strangely familiar. His fault. His decisions had caused this. He'd gotten his way. Convinced her to go even though she didn't want to. Convinced her they could outrun the storm. Was he never going to learn? He was like some kind of spoiled two-year-old always insisting on getting his way. And his way always seemed to have dire consequences. He had no business dragging Julie to the island.

He heard a knock at the door and went to open it.

"Hi." Susan stood in the doorway. "Just wanted to let you know I went and got Julie and brought her home. She's all settled in at her house if you want to go visit her."

"How is she doing?"

"Well, she's arguing about taking it easy, of course. But I fixed her some lunch and I'm hoping she'll stay put." Susan looked at him expectantly. "So, are you going to go see her?"

Reed stood silently, his thoughts rolling around in his mind.

Susan shifted her weight and looked directly into his eyes. A frown creased her forehead. "You are going over?"

He sighed. A deep sigh that seemed to come from somewhere so far inside that it tore through him and made his heart ache. "I... am. I need to talk to her."

"Okay..." Her voice drifted off and she looked at him like she didn't totally trust him.

She turned and walked away down the hallway, and he watched her measured steps. Julie was lucky to have such a good friends as Tally and Susan. They would be there for her... after he talked to her.

Reed stood beside Julie's couch, watching her sleep. The bandage on her head mocked him, reminding him of the pain he'd caused her. What if it had been worse? He couldn't bear to think about that. This was bad enough.

Julie stirred and opened her eyes. A smile spread across her face when she saw him. "Reed, you're here."

He moved the tray down and perched on the edge of the sturdy coffee table. He took her hands in his. "We need to talk."

"We do. I have something I need to tell you." She pushed up and sat on the couch.

He held up a hand to stop her. He needed to just get this over with. "I… I'm leaving."

"What?" Her eyes flew open wide.

"It's time for me to get back to my real life. We've always known it was going to happen."

"But you still have another week, at least."

"Julie, I'm sorry. Sorry about everything. The accident. Insisting you go to the island with me. Everything. I should have listened to you about the storm, too. I never learn my lesson. I keep repeating history. I'm sorry."

"But, this isn't your fault."

"I just can't keep doing this. I make the same mistake over and over and people get hurt."

"Reed, it was an *accident*. And I had one of most wonderful afternoons of my life with you on the island."

239

Her words tore at his heart. He'd had the best time with her, too. He could almost still feel her in his arms. Feel her lips against his. But there was no way he was going to endanger someone again. The fates were laughing at him for thinking he even had a chance at love again.

Love?

He pushed that thought right from his mind.

Her eyes took on a haunted look and she pulled back from him. "You're leaving me, aren't you? Nothing I say will make you change your mind."

"I have to go. I'm sorry to hurt you." His heart burned in his chest, and he could barely take a breath.

"Leave then. Go. I won't stop you. I won't even try."

He stood up, looking down at her. Tears began to fill her eyes, but he could tell she was valiantly fighting them off.

"I am sorry. I wish… Well, I'm sorry."

He turned and walked out her door and out of her life.

CHAPTER 24

Tally sat with her arm around Julie, handing her tissues to dry her tears. "It's going to be okay."

"I should have known better. What was I thinking? I was such a fool. Why did I think I could trust him?" Julie choked out her words.

"There is nothing wrong with taking a chance on love."

"I *don't* love him," Julie insisted. "I just thought I did."

"He's afraid. You can see how he felt history was repeating itself. And I know you're afraid of being rejected, of being left, but you love him. I can see it in your eyes."

"I don't."

Tally could see she was getting nowhere with Julie. The woman was hurt. Hurt deeply. Both she and Reed were fools. Throwing away a chance at love because they were both afraid of repeating their past.

"You should go talk to him. Convince him he's wrong."

"I can't do that. I just… can't. I thought that maybe, just maybe, he was *the one*. I know we've only known each other a few weeks, but I thought… well, it doesn't matter what I thought. If he doesn't want to be with me, there is nothing I can do about it. Besides, I'll never, ever trust him again. I'll never let him get close enough to hurt me again… to leave me."

"Love is worth fighting for, you know."

"He doesn't *want* me."

"He does, he's just afraid."

Julie looked at her. "I'm afraid, too. Afraid of what life is going to be like without him."

Tally sat with her friend, comforting her. Tally knew, better than most, that you should never throw away a chance at true love, because it rarely came around twice.

Reed stood at the end of the bed, tossing things into his suitcase. He now knew what the term heartbroken meant. He felt like his heart was shattering into a million pieces. He'd caused Julie so much pain. That was last thing he'd wanted to do, but he'd seen it in her eyes. The pain, the hurt, the distrust.

How did everything get so messed up? She'd be better off without him anyway. He'd always planned to head back to Seattle, he was just leaving a bit early. He couldn't stay here on Belle Island. It wasn't fair to her... and he was pretty sure he wasn't strong enough to see her again.

The problem was, he knew the one thing Julie didn't need was more rejection in her life, and yet, that was exactly what he'd given her. He threw a handful of shirts into the suitcase in a jumbled mess. Not that he cared. He didn't care about anything right now except for getting out of this town. Forget everything about the last few weeks and everyone he'd met.

A sharp rap at the door drew his attention. He strode over to the door and jerked it open with more force than he intended.

Tally stood there with a look of such... *fire*... in her eyes. "We're going to talk." Tally pushed passed him and stepped into the room.

"I—"

"No, I want you to listen." Tally spun around and pointed a finger at him. "You know you broke her heart, right?"

"I—"

"I just want to make sure you know how deeply you hurt her. She'd started to trust you. To think there was something between you two… which, by the way, is evident to anyone who looks at you two. There is something there."

Tally walked over to the bed and stared down at the clothes spilling out of the suitcase. "I see you're leaving."

"I thought it best."

Tally looked at him, straight into his eyes, straight into his soul. "I think… you should reconsider. I know you somehow have Julie's accident wrapped up in your guilt over your wife's accident. But you know what, life sometimes just throws tough curves at us. Things we don't want to deal with, or live through. You can run away and hide, afraid to take chances… or you can square your shoulders, deal with it and embrace the life you've been given."

He slumped into a chair as her words struck a chord deep within his heart.

Tally walked over and sat in the chair beside him. "It's obvious you love her." She reached out and touched his arm. "You do, don't you?"

He looked into those kind eyes. "… I do." He realized with a start, that he did truly love Julie, not that he'd been able to admit it to himself before this.

He raked his hands through his hair. "I've really messed this up, haven't I?"

"Yes, you have. The question now is, what are you going to do about it?"

"I… don't know how to fix it. She'll never trust

me again, and I wouldn't blame her. I've been so wrapped up in my guilt, in my own version of reality. I feel so badly about Julie getting hurt. If only I hadn't pushed her into going…"

"So, are you going to beat yourself up for the rest of your life? Blame yourself for every accident? Walk away from a good woman just to hide out and lick your wounds?"

"I don't know what to do."

"Do you want to be with her?"

Reed looked across the room and back to Tally. "I do. More than anything in the world."

"Then, I suggest you come up with a really grand apology, tell her how you feel about her, and beg her to give you another chance. Beg her to trust you."

Reed jumped up. "Will you help me?"

"I'd do anything for Julie."

"I've got an idea, but I need some help…"

"You got it."

CHAPTER 25

"I don't really feel like going anywhere tonight." Julie picked up a tray of dirty dishes as she cleared off a table in The Sweet Shoppe.

"You've done nothing but work and go straight home and mope for days now. Come out with Tally and me. We're going to barbecue at Sunset Cove. Just a few friends. A small get-together for Tally's birthday. It will do you good to get out." Susan followed Julie around as she cleared another table.

"I don't know." Though Julie felt a wave of guilt for even considering missing Tally's birthday. But she just didn't feel like being around people or going to a party.

"Great. I'll pick you up at six."

"I didn't say I'd go." Julie set the tray down on a table. "I just... I'm not up for it. I wouldn't be very good company."

"You don't need to be. You know that Tally will be disappointed if you don't come."

"She'd understand."

"Okay, you're right. She would. But she'd still be disappointed. You don't want that, do you?" Susan nailed her with a look that made Julie squirm.

"You've got that you're-so-disappointing-me look down pat."

"I've had years of perfecting it on Jamie when he was growing up." Susan grinned.

"You sure are persistent." Julie still didn't feel like going, but she knew she should. She couldn't bear to disappoint Tally. She'd almost forgotten it was her birthday. She'd have to run out and get her a gift, too.

"I am persistent. One of my many charming qualities."

Julie laughed. "You win. I'll go. I guess you're right that I can't just mope around forever."

Reed had spent the last few days trying to make everything perfect for tonight. He'd found solar holiday lights and strung them around the trees at the cove Tally had told him about and placed hurricane lanterns with candles for the tables by the barbecue pit. He'd helped plan the meal with Tally and gotten a balloon bouquet for Tally's birthday. He tied it to one of the Adirondack chairs on the beach.

He'd gone over and over what words he could say to Julie, how he could convince her this one last time that he really was over his past and he'd never leave her again. He worked on every little detail he could think of to show her how serious he was.

He stood on Lighthouse Point and looked out at the ocean. It was probably wrong to press his luck and make another wish, but he leaned down and picked up a perfect shell resting at his feet.

The wind blew in gently and the sun warmed his face. He closed his eyes and made his wish.

"I wish... I hope... that I can persuade Julie to take me back."

He opened his eyes and threw the shell out into the ocean in a perfect arc. It plunked into the sea, along with his wish.

Now, tonight, he'd see if his wish came true.

Tally walked up to the cove and looked around in amazement. Reed had outdone himself. The picnic area was surrounded by twinkling holiday lights, the table had a lace tablecloth and flowers on it. He'd lined the Adirondack chairs up facing the beach.

Paul and Josephine were already there, chatting with Jamie.

"Well, did you convince Julie to come?" Paul gave

Tally a hug. Tally was glad they'd let Paul and Josephine in on their plans.

"I think so. Susan guilted her into it, but she's coming."

Tally was not above using her own birthday to coax Julie into coming to the beach. It was all part of the plan. A plan that she hoped worked. Julie was a stubborn one though, and she'd warned Reed that she'd do everything in her power to help him, but she could make no promises.

"Do you think Reed's plan will work?" Josephine's face showed concern.

"I know he's spent days working on it. I hope so. It would be a shame to see Julie miss this chance. I know she's afraid of rejection. I get that. Both of those two have a lot of baggage to deal with. But, it is just obvious that they are in love, even if they don't admit it to themselves or to each other."

"I think she's going to be hard to convince." Paul shook his head.

"I think she needs to take a leap of faith just this once. I truly think Reed has made peace with his past, now Julie needs to do the same." Tally sighed. "And I'm just the person to help Reed put his plan into play."

Jamie walked up and hugged her. "Happy birthday, Tally."

"Thanks, Jamie. Glad you could come."

"Who can say no to Mom?" Jamie grinned. "Not

that I'd miss your birthday, anyway. I've got burgers and brats on the grill."

"Sounds good." Tally looked around at the charming setup Reed had arranged at the cove. "I just hope this works. You know, the best birthday present I could get would be for Julie and Reed to sort this all out. I just want that girl to be happy. When I see those two together? I'm pretty sure—no I'm *positive*—they are meant to be together."

He paced back and forth down the beach from the cove, out of sight of the birthday party guests. Now it was just up to Tally and Susan to get Julie to actually come to the party, then it was all up to him.

Apprehension coursed through him and he glanced at his watch. He paced down the beach again, reciting words in his mind, still uncertain he'd be able to convince her, to assure he'd never, ever leave her. He glanced at his watch again, it was time.

He walked back to his bike, climbed on, and rode around the bend and entered the cove. He leaned his bike against an old dune fence. With determined strides, he joined the group. He could see Julie standing with her friends. He swiped a hand at his hair, brushing it back—he still hadn't gotten that haircut he needed. Why he was thinking about haircuts at a time like this was beyond him. He kept walking. Closer. Closer.

He saw the exact moment that Julie spotted him. She dropped her soda can to the beach. She quickly leaned over and picked it up as he approached.

"What's he doing here?" Julie's voice was steely cold.

"Julie, I didn't think you'd come if I asked to see you." Reed stood in front of Julie.

"And you'd be right."

Jamie, Paul, and Josephine moved a bit of a distance away to the chairs. Susan and Tally held their place. No doubt ready to catch Julie if she started to run away... or maybe it was to back her up if she hauled off and punched him...

"I'm so sorry. I know you've heard me say it before. I was just so shocked when it happened again. I convinced you to go somewhere you didn't really want to go... and then you got hurt. It was like I was repeating the accident with... Victoria." He cleared his throat and took a step closer to Julie.

"I was... afraid. Afraid I'd lost you, too. That's no excuse though. It was cowardly and wrong. I should have faced my fears." He turned toward Tally. "Tally made me see that. Hiding away from things that frighten us is no way to live and I don't want live that way any longer."

Julie took a slight step backwards, as he took another step closer. And another.

"I'm trying to make peace with everything. Tally has driven me to Sarasota each day and I've taken driving lessons with someone who specializes in people who know how to drive, but some trauma has made it hard for them. I'm getting better. I'm dealing with it."

He took a few quick steps back to his bike and grabbed a bouquet of flowers from the basket. He walked back over to Julie and extended them towards her.

"Look. Yellow flowers. I'm not afraid of yellow anymore, either. Who knew you could conquer a fear of color?" He flashed her a quick smile. "I know these yellow roses are your favorite."

Julie reached for the flowers, which was more than he expected. His hand brushed hers as she took them from him. A jolt of electricity raced through him, giving him hope.

"I'm willing to take as long as you need to convince you I'm here to stay. I've talked to my company, and I'm going to try working remotely from Belle Island. I'll have to travel back to Seattle once a month or so, but otherwise, I'm going to be here."

Julie's eyes flickered like glittering emeralds, but he still couldn't tell if she was wavering, if she'd take him back. If she could let herself trust him one more time.

He took a deep breath and continued. "I know we've only known each other for less than a month, but for me... well, I know I want to spend the rest of my life with you." His heart pounded in his chest. If this didn't convince her he was serious about staying with her, nothing would. He dropped to one knee. "I love you Julie Farmington, and I want to marry you. To spend all my days with you. I think I knew you were the one the first time I saw you in that stained t-shirt on the steps to the inn, with the sea breeze tossing your hair all round. You looked into my eyes and I was... taken. Right that very moment."

"Oh." Julie gasped a tiny breath.

He knelt on the sand, holding out the ring box, waiting for an answer.

"Reed..." Julie looked to Tally standing beside her.

"Love is always worth the risk." Tally whispered and nodded.

Julie looked back to Reed. "I think it's crazy that we've only known each other such a short time, but I feel like I've known you forever. I've missed you these last days... I've felt like, I don't know... half. Half-alive. Half a person. Just... half. You've done so much to show me how you've changed, to help me believe you'll stay. Make me feel like... we belong together."

Hope fluttered through Reed. "We do belong together."

Julie knelt in the sand in front of him and looked straight into his soul. "We do belong together. Yes, I'll marry you, Newman, Reed Newman." Julie laughed a symphony of magical tones.

He hugged her, then slipped the ring on her finger. "You've made me very, very happy. I promise I'll never leave, never give you a reason to fear you'll be left behind. We'll be a family, you and I."

A family. She was finally going to get the family she'd wanted her whole life. Julie looked at the sparkling emerald on her finger, the perfect stone for her engagement. Tears trailed down her cheeks, but she didn't bother to wipe them away. Joy flowed through her, blossoming into a perfect feeling of contentment.

She looked over at Tally and Susan. Susan was wiping away tears of her own, and Tally's eyes shone with pleasure.

She turned her face up to Reed's. "I love you. So very, very much."

"I love you, too. I plan on making you happy to the end of our days." Reed leaned down and pressed a gentle kiss to her lips. He stood up, reached down a hand, and pulled her to her feet. He released her into the warm hugs of her friends Susan and Tally.

Tally whispered in her ear. "You've made me proud. Tackled your fear and moved past it. I'm very happy for you. Reed is a good man."

Julie hugged her friend back and looked over

Tally's shoulder at Reed, who was being congratulated by Jamie, Paul, and Josephine.

She looked around the enchanted cove and knew that she'd never, ever forget this moment. The day she said yes to marrying her soul mate and found a family of her own.

CHAPTER 26

Tally, Susan, and Julie sat having coffee at the bakery at end of the breakfast rush—that was no longer a rush these days. Julie looked up and saw Camille and Delbert come through the door.

Julie thought Camille had some nerve to come into the bakery with Delbert for their breakfast, but she stopped short of telling them to leave. She didn't want to make a scene in front of her other customers.

Camille walked over to where they were sitting. "The sheriff said to meet him here."

"He's not here." Julie wondered what this was all about.

"I guess we'll have something to eat while we wait." Camille sounded reluctant.

Not any more reluctant than Julie felt about serving her.

The door opened and the sheriff stepped inside.

He crossed over to them. "Good, I see you're all here. I've got news." He flipped open his ever-present notebook. "I've caught the thief."

"You have?" Camille's eyes widen. "It's not Julie?"

"No, ma'am. It's the pool boy you hired. Got a tip from a…" Sheriff Dave looked at his note. "A Reed Newman."

"Reed?"

"Yes, ma'am. He suggested we check out the pool service and the gardening service. Appears the pool service hired this new worker. We've had reports of stolen items from two other customers of the pool service you use. Caught him red handed. We've recovered your mother's things."

"That's wonderful news." Camille clapped her hands and turned to Julie. "No hard feelings, right? I never really believed it was you."

Julie didn't even dignify Camille with an answer.

"No, of course you didn't." Tally rolled her eyes.

"This is fortunate, because Mama is having a party this weekend and her caterer just quit at the last minute. You'll help us out won't you? You'll cater the party for Mama?"

"No." Julie, Tally, and Susan said in unison.

"Well… I never." Camille's face turned red and she turned to the sheriff. "Thanks for your help, Sheriff. I'll tell Mama what a good job you did."

"It was all because of that Reed fellow."

"Whatever." Camille turned away. "Come on Delbert, let's go eat somewhere else."

Delbert flashed them an apologetic look and trailed after Camille. The couple walked out the door with the sheriff.

"Well, that's good news." Tally took a sip of her coffee.

"I had no idea Reed was working on trying to figure out who really stole all the things." Julie sat, stunned by the turn of events.

"You've got yourself a good man." Susan smiled.

"I do. And I have Tally to thank for that. If she hadn't talked some sense into both of us, we would have let our chance for happiness slip by."

Tally reached over and squeezed her hand. "That's all I've ever wanted for you, Julie. Since that very first day I met you, that scared, lost girl trying to stay dry out by my storage shed." Tally smiled. "You've become quite the woman, and I'm proud of you."

A wave of joy and contentment swept through Julie. She *belonged* here, with these women, in this town. She had the respect of Tally, the friendship of both of these women, and… she had Reed's love.

Life didn't get much better.

Reed and Julie stood on the beach at the water's edge at Lighthouse Point. His arm rested gently around her as they watched the setting sun. She turned her face up to his and he leaned down and gently kissed her lips.

"I love you." He whispered the words against her cheek.

"I love you, too." She leaned against him.

She looked down at the sand and a bright golden shell tumbled at their feet. She reached down and scooped it up. She turned the shell over and over in her hand, then pressed it into Reed's palm.

"Should we make a wish?"

"What should we wish for?" His eyes were filled with a love she could feel to her very being. A love she trusted.

Julie took a deep breath. "We wish for... a long life filled with love and happiness."

"That is a perfect wish," Reed added.

Reed took her hand in his, and together they tossed the shell into the ocean.

THANK YOU for reading my story. I hope you enjoyed it. Sign up for my newsletter to be updated with information on new releases, promotions, and giveaways. The signup is at my website, kaycorrell.com.

Reviews help other readers find new books. I always appreciate when my readers take time to leave an honest review.

I love to hear from my readers. Feel free to contact me at authorcontact@kaycorrell.com

COMFORT CROSSING ~ THE SERIES

The Shop on Main - Book One

The Memory Box - Book Two

The Christmas Cottage - A Holiday Novella (Book 2.5)

The Letter - Book Three

The Christmas Scarf - A Holiday Novella (Book 3.5)

The Magnolia Cafe - Book Four

The Unexpected Wedding - Book Five

The Wedding in the Grove (crossover short story between series - Josephine and Paul from The Letter.)

LIGHTHOUSE POINT ~ THE SERIES

Wish Upon a Shell - Book One

Wedding on the Beach - Book Two

Love at the Lighthouse - Book Three

Cottage near the Point - Book Four

Return to the Island - Book Five

INDIGO BAY ~ a multi-author series of sweet romance

Sweet Sunrise - Book Three

Sweet Holiday Memories - A short holiday story

Sweet Starlight - Book Nine

ABOUT THE AUTHOR

Kay writes sweet, heartwarming stories that are a cross between women's fiction and contemporary romance. She is known for her charming small towns, quirky townsfolk, and enduring strong friendships between the women in her books.

Kay lives in the Midwest of the U.S. and can often be found out and about with her camera, taking a myriad of photographs which she likes to incorporate into her book covers. When not lost in her writing or photography, she can be found spending time with her ever-supportive husband, knitting, working in her garden, or playing with her puppies—two cavaliers and one naughty but adorable Australian shepherd. Kay and her husband also love to travel. When it comes to vacation time, she is torn between a nice trip to the beach or the mountains—but the mountains only get considered in the summer—she swears she's allergic to snow.

Learn more about Kay and her books at
kaycorrell.com

While you're there, sign up for her newsletter to hear
about new releases, sales, and giveaways.

WHERE TO FIND ME:
kaycorrell.com
authorcontact@kaycorrell.com

Join my Facebook Reader Group. We have lots of fun
and you'll hear about sales and new releases first!
https://www.facebook.com/groups/KayCorrell/

Made in the USA
Coppell, TX
18 April 2021

53982072R00163